W9-BIB-233

The
Rainmaker

A ROMANTIC COMEDY IN THREE ACTS

by

N. Richard Nash

SAMUEL
FRENCH

FOUNDED 1830

New York Hollywood London Toronto
SAMUELFRENCH.COM

Copyright © 1954, 1955, 1982, 1983 by N. Richard Nash

ALL RIGHTS RESERVED

CAUTION: Professionals and amateurs are hereby warned that *THE RAINMAKER* is subject to a royalty. It is fully protected under the copyright laws of the United States of America, the British Commonwealth, including Canada, and all other countries of the Copyright Union. All rights, including professional, amateur, motion picture, recitation, lecturing, public reading, radio broadcasting, television and the rights of translation into foreign languages are strictly reserved. In its present form the play is dedicated to the reading public only.

The amateur live stage performance rights to *THE RAINMAKER* are controlled exclusively by Samuel French, Inc., and royalty arrangements and licenses must be secured well in advance of presentation. PLEASE NOTE that amateur royalty fees are set upon application in accordance with your producing circumstances. When applying for a royalty quotation and license please give us the number of performances intended, dates of production, your seating capacity and admission fee. Royalties are payable one week before the opening performance of the play to Samuel French, Inc., at 45 W. 25th Street, New York, NY 10010.

Royalty of the required amount must be paid whether the play is presented for charity or gain and whether or not admission is charged.

Stock royalty quoted upon application to Samuel French, Inc.

For all other rights than those stipulated above, apply to William Morris Agency, Inc., 1325 Avenue of the Americas, New York, NY 10019.

Particular emphasis is laid on the question of amateur or professional readings, permission and terms for which must be secured in writing from Samuel French, Inc.

Copying from this book in whole or in part is strictly forbidden by law, and the right of performance is not transferable.

Whenever the play is produced the following notice must appear on all programs, printing and advertising for the play: "Produced by special arrangement with Samuel French, Inc."

Due authorship credit must be given on all programs, printing and advertising for the play.

No one shall commit or authorize any act or omission by which the copyright of, or the right to copyright, this play may be impaired.

No one shall make any changes in this play for the purpose of production.

Publication of this play does not imply availability for performance. Both amateurs and professionals considering a production are strongly advised in their own interests to apply to Samuel French, Inc., for written permission before starting rehearsals, advertising, or booking a theatre.

No part of this book may be reproduced, stored in a retrieval system, or transmitted in any form, by any means, now known or yet to be invented, including mechanical, electronic, photocopying, recording, videotaping, or otherwise, without the prior written permission of the publisher.

ISBN **978-0-573-61461-3**   Printed in U.S.A.   #104

For

J E G J

who know who they are

and know how they are loved

Sound effects cassette tape available
@ $32.50, plus postage.

THE RAINMAKER

STORY OF THE PLAY

(6 males; 1 female)

At the time of a paralyzing drought in the West, we discover a girl whose father and two brothers are worried as much about her becoming an old maid as they are about their dying cattle. For the truth is, she is indeed a plain girl. The brothers try every possible scheme to marry her off, but without success. Nor is there any sign of relief from the dry heat. When suddenly from out of nowhere appears a picaresque character with a mellifluous tongue and the most grandiose notions a man could imagine. He is a rainmaker, and he promises to bring rain, for $100. It's a whacky idea, but the rainmaker is so refreshing and ingratiating that the family finally consent. Forthwith they begin banging on big bass drums to rattle the sky; while the rainmaker turns his magic on the girl, and persuades her that she has a very real beauty of her own. And she believes it, just as her father believes the fellow can actually bring rain. And rain does come, and so does love. "A cloudburst of a hit."—*N.Y. World Telegram & Sun.* "Admirable skill . . . Insight into the human heart . . . the touch of a poet . . . A hit you must see."—*N.Y. Mirror.* An excellent play for all groups.

FOREWORD

When drought hits the lush grasslands of the richly fertile west, they are green no more and the dying is a palpable thing. What happens to verdure and vegetation, to cattle and livestock can be read in the coldly statistical little bulletins freely issued by the Department of Agriculture. What happens to the people of the west—beyond the calculable and terrible phenomena of sudden poverty and loss of substance—is an incalculable and febrile kind of desperation. Rain will never come again; the earth will be sere forever; and in all of heaven, there is no promise of remedy.

Yet, men of wisdom like H. C. Curry know to be patient with heaven. They know that the earth will not thirst forever; they know that one day they will again awaken to a green morning. Young people like Lizzie, his daughter, cannot know this as certainly as he does. Bright as she is, she cannot know. She can only count the shooting stars, and hope.

The play is set in such a drought-beset region in the moment when Lizzie's hope is faltering. Because the hopes of Lizzie and H.C., of Jim and Starbuck and File are finally brought to blessing, because the people of the play are deserving and filled with love of one another—and most important, because it is not always that the hopes of deserving, loving human beings *are* blessed—this play is a comedy and it is a romance. It must never be forgotten that it is a romance, never for an instant by the director, the actors, the scenic designer or the least-sung usher in the Forrest Theatre in Philadelphia.

In this regard there must be, without eschewing truth, a kind of romantic beauty in the relationships of all the characters with one another. Especially so in the Curry

5

family, even when Noah is laying down the stern law of a rigid God who, to Noah, looks rather like an irate Certified Public Accountant. There must be love in the house, or somewhere a benign promise.

This same felicity in the sets. True, the Curry ranch house—the living and dining rooms, the kitchen—is a place where people scratch their heads and take their shoes off, where woodwork has to be scrubbed and pots scoured. But more important, it is a place where beauty is made out of affection and all manner of gentleness. The tack room, if seen realistically, might be a dust bin attractive only to the termites and the rodents of the night. But if the designer sees it romantically—as Lizzie might see it, with all its memorabilia of childhood—it will tell the hopeful promise intended. Or File's office— it is not an office really, although File's rolltop desk is there and his old fashioned telephone—it is File's secret hiding place from the world, the island where he errantly believes he can bring balm to his loneliness.

Despite the mention of many playing areas, it is essential that this be a one-set play. The center stage area should be the house—the living room or "parlor" as they called it in those days, combined with dining and kitchen areas into one large playing space, taking up perhaps half the stage. Down right, File's office, approximately a quarter of the stage—and down left, the tack room, the remaining quarter. It is essential that it be a one-set play—not for reasons of production economy, although economies will fortuitously flow from it—but because the designer can best serve the unity intended if the visual effects seem to be closely related and unified. And in the same regard—to avoid time separations as well as spatial ones—there must be no lowering of a curtain between scenes—merely a dimming of light in one area and a lift in light in another.

If there is incidental music in the play, it should sing on the romantic instruments and forswear brass and tympani. It should lament on strings and woodwins and promise sweet melody.

Perhaps the best rule of thumb in direction, acting, scenery, music is this oversimplification: Let us not use the panoramic lenses. Let us focus closely, but through a romantically gauzed lens, on the face of Lizzie's loneliness, and on her hope. Life can be seen deeply through small lenses. And truthfully even through gauze.

Copy of the program of THE RAINMAKER as produced
at The Cort Theatre, New York, October 28, 1954:

Ethel Linder Reiner
in association with
Hope Abelson
presents
Geraldine Page
in

THE RAINMAKER

a romantic play
by N. Richard Nash
with
Darren McGavin   Richard Coogan   Joseph Sullivan
Albert Salmi   Tom Flatley Reynolds
and
Cameron Prud'homme
Direction by Joseph Anthony
Setting and Lighting by Ralph Alswang
Costumes by Bolasni

CAST

(in order of appearance)

H. C. CURRY .... *Cameron Prud'homme*
NOAH CURRY .... *Joseph Sullivan*
JIM CURRY .... *Albert Salmi*
LIZZIE CURRY .... *Geraldine Page*
FILE .... *Richard Coogan*
SHERIFF THOMAS .... *Tom Flatley Reynolds*
BILL STARBUCK .... *Darren McGavin*

SYNOPSIS OF SCENES

The play takes place in a western state on a summer day in a time of drought.

ACT ONE

Day.

ACT TWO

That evening.

ACT THREE

Later the same night.

The Rainmaker

ACT ONE

*The LIGHTS come up slowly to reveal the Center area
of the stage which is the interior of the Curry house.
The Curry ranch is a prosperous one and the house
is a place where gentle, kindly people who have an
uneducated but profoundly true sense of beauty
have lived in love of one another. It is strongly
masculine in its basic structure—brick and hand
hewn beams and such—but it shows Lizzie's hand
in many of its appointments. We see a comfortable
kitchen on the Left; the rest of the downstairs living
area is a combination of living and dining room. One
of the earliest telephones on the wall; a gramophone
with a horn; a primitive radio, a crystal set which,
when operated, sets up a fearful screech of static.
There are stairs Left to the bedrooms and a large,
imposing front door up Right to the private road
that leads to the main highway. (See scene design
at back.)*

*It is early morning of a scorching, drought-ridden day.
Already the blazing sun has taken over the house.*

When the lights are up we see H. C. CURRY *making breakfast. He is in his mid-fifties, powerfully set, capable,
a good man to take store in. But he's not all prosaic
efficiency—there's a dream in him. A moment, then
his oldest son,* NOAH, *comes in up Right from outdoors. He is somewhat like his father, without* H.C.'s
*imagination. As a matter of fact, he has little
imagination at all—a somewhat self-righteous man,
rigidly opinionated. He carries a saddle.*

NOAH. That you, Pop?

H.C. Yeah. Mornin', Noah.

NOAH. I heard somebody fussin' around in the kitchen.
—I was hopin' it was Lizzie. *(Puts saddle on floor by chest.)*

H.C. She was so dead beat after her trip I figured I'd let her sleep.

NOAH. Yeah. I heard her walkin' her room last night until hell knows when. *(Looking at his pocket watch.)* Gettin' late. Maybe I better wake her up. *(He starts for the stairs.)*

H.C. *(To Left Center.)* No—don't do that, Noah. She must of had a pretty rough time. Let her sleep it off. *(Sits down Center.)*

NOAH. I was sure hopin' she'd cook breakfast. *(Then, quickly, with a half smile, so as not to offend H.C.)* But I guess if we didn't croak after a week of your cookin', we can live through another meal. *(Goes to the radio and fiddles with it. It screeches.)*

H.C. Noah—Jimmy just fixed that thing—don't you go breakin' it again.

NOAH. If that kid's gonna waste his money on a darnfool crystal set—why can't we get some good out of it? —Can't hear a thing.

H.C. What do you want to hear?

NOAH. Thought somebody'd say somethin' about the drought.

H.C. Only one thing to say. No rain.

NOAH. *(Switching off the set)* And no sign of it neither. *(He goes to the calendar alongside of which hangs a pencil on a string.)* Well, cross out another day.

H.C. Noah, I wish you wouldn't do that— *(Rises; to kitchen door.)* You and that damn calendar. Why'n't you stop countin'? When it rains, it rains!

NOAH. You know what I seen this mornin'? *(To cupboard for ledgers.)* Three more calves down and out— and a couple of heifers! And you know what I had to do? I had to give Sandy and Frank their time.

H.C. *(Disturbed.)* You mean you fired them?

NOAH. No—I just laid 'em off—till the drought's over.

H.C. You shouldn't of done that, Noah.

NOAH. Listen, Pop—if you want to take over the bookkeepin', you're welcome to it. *(Taking two large black ledgers off the cupboard.)* Here's the books—you can have 'em! *(To Right of table; sits.)*

H.C. *(Left of table. With a smile)* Now I wouldn't do that to you, Noah. How do you want your eggs?

NOAH. What's the best way you can't ruin 'em?

H.C. Raw!

NOAH. *(Crosses down and sits on hassock.)* I'll take 'em raw!

(JIM CURRY comes racing downstairs. JIM is the youngest in the family, in his early twenties—but he's big and broad shouldered and looks older until he opens his mouth; then he's a child. He isn't very bright and this is his great cross. He is filled with inchoate longing. At the moment he is agog with excitement, as he nearly always is; but right now his frenzy has to do with universal catastrophe.)

JIM. Mornin'! Mornin', Pop!

H.C. *and* NOAH. Mornin', Jimmy— Mornin'.

JIM. Pop! Pop, it's like I said yesterday—just like I told you!

H.C. What'd you tell me, Jim? *(Exits Left.)*

JIM. *(Putting on shoes down Center)* I said to you like this, I said: "Pop the whole world's gonna blow up!" I said: "The world's gonna get all s-w-o-l-e up—and bust right in our faces!"

H.C. *(Enters to get plate from cupboard and exits Left.)* You sure of that, Jimmy?

JIM. You bet I'm sure. You see it's all got to do with the spots on the sun. One of these days them spots is gonna get so big the sun won't be able to shine through! *(Crosses Right to porch.)* And then, brother—bang!

(H.C. re-enters.)

NOAH. *(Rises; takes plate from* H.C.; *sits Right of table.)* You keep thinkin' about that you're gonna miss your breakfast.

JIM. *(To Center.)* Yeah. Ain't no good thinkin' about it—it just gets me all upset. *(Noticing* NOAH's *food. Sits Left of table.)* Holy mackerel, Noah—them eggs is raw!

NOAH. What of it?

JIM. What's the matter—you sick?

NOAH. No, I ain't sick.

JIM. You sure must be sick if you're eatin' raw eggs.

H.C. *(Above Center.)* He's all right, Jim He just don't like my cookin'.

JIM. Why? You cook better'n Lizzie. I like the way you cook, Pop. Everything slides down nice and greasy.

H.C. *(Wryly accepting the dubious compliment.)* Thanks, Jim. How do you want your eggs? *(Exits Left.)*

JIM Oh any old way.

H.C. How many?

JIM. *(Casually)* I guess five or six'll do. (JIM *has already begun to gorge on bread and jam.)*

NOAH. Jimmy—

JIM. *(Bolting his food—not looking up)* Huh?

NOAH. Jimmy, if you'll come up for a minute, I got somethin' to say to you.

JIM. What?

NOAH. Last night— You coulda got yourself into a hatful of trouble.

(H.C. *enters to Left of* JIM.)

JIM. *(Embarrassed to discuss it in front of his father.)* Do we have to talk about it now?

H.C. *(Crosses up Center.)* What kind of trouble, Noah?

NOAH. *(Distastefully)* A certain girl named Snookie.

H.C. Oh—was Snookie at the dance? *(To above sofa.)*

NOAH. Was she at the dance?—You'da thought nobody *else* was there! She comes drivin' up in a brand new five cylinder Essex car! And her hair is so bleach-blonde—

JIM. It ain't bleached!

NOAH. Don't tell me! Gil Demby says she comes into the store and buys a pint of peroxide every month!

JIM. What's that? I use peroxide for a cut finger!

NOAH. If she got cut that often she'd bleed to death!

H.C. *(Quietly)* What happened, Jim?

NOAH. I'll tell you what happened! Along about nine-thirty I look around. No Jim—and no Snookie. That dumb kid—he walked outta that barn dance without even tippin' his hat.

(H.C. *to kitchen, takes off apron.*)

And he went off with that hot pants girl!

JIM. I didn't go off with her—I went off by myself. I walked outside and I was lookin' at that Essex. And pretty soon she comes out and she's kinda starin' me up and down. And I says to her: "How many cylinders has this Essex got?" And she says: "Five." And then she says to me: "How tall are you?" And I says: "Six." And before you know it we're ridin' in the Essex and she's got that car racin' forty miles an hour! Man, it was fast!

NOAH. Everything about her is fast!

JIM. *(Rearing)* Whatta you mean by that, Noah?

(H.C. *enters with two plates.*)

NOAH. Just what I said!

(To H.C., *who sits above* Center.*)*

When the dance was over—when we were all supposed to go pick Lizzie up at the depot—I had to go lookin' for him! And you know where he was? He was sittin' in that girl's car—parked outside of Demby's store— and the two of them—I never seen such carryin's on! They were so twisted up together, I couldn't tell where he left off and Snookie began! If I hadn't of come along, hell knows what would of happened!

JIM. *(Tragically)* Yeah—hell knows— I could of come home with her little red hat.

H.C. With her what?

NOAH. She wears a little red hat.

H.C. Well, why would you come home with her little red hat?

JIM. Nothin'—nothin'.

NOAH. Go on—tell him.

JIM. Noah—you quit it!

NOAH. Well, I'll tell him! She always wears this little red hat. And last night, Dumbo Hopkinson says to her: "Snookie, you gonna wear that little red hat all your life?" And she giggles and says: "Well, I hope not, Dumbo! I'm gonna give it to some handsome fella—when, as and if!"

(As H.C. smiles.)

It ain't funny, Pop! *(To JIM.)* Do you know what trouble you can get yourself into with a girl like that? A dumb kid like you—why, pretty soon she's got you hog-tied and you have to marry her!

JIM. Why don't you let me alone!

NOAH. *(Outraged.)* Did you hear that, Pop?

H.C. Maybe it's a good idea, Noah.

NOAH. What's a good idea?

H.C. To let him alone.

JIM. Maybe it is!

NOAH. *(Hurt; in high dudgeon. Rises to kitchen for coffee pot.)* All right! If you want me to let you alone—Kid, you're alone!

JIM. *(Withdrawing a little.)* I don't know what you're gettin' so mad about.

NOAH. *(Re-enters. Pours coffee.)* You don't huh? You think I *like* lookin' out for you? Well I don't! Taggin' after me all your life! "How do I tie my shoelaces? How do I do long division?" Well, if you don't want me to give you no advice—if you think you're so smart—

JIM. I ain't sayin' I'm so smart. Heck, I don't mind you tellin' me how to do and how to figure things out—

NOAH. *(Bitingly)* Thanks! *(Sits.)*

JIM. What I mean—I appreciate it. *(Bellowing)* I just wish you wouldn't holler!

H.C. *(Rises.)* All right—that's enough, boys! *(A*

moment. H.C. *goes to the thermometer on porch.)* A hundred and one degrees.

NOAH. If only it'd cool off at night.

JIM. *(Rises.)* I don't mind a hot night. *(Longingly)* Somethin' about a hot night— Gets you kind of —well— all stirred up inside. Why didn't Lizzie come down and make our breakfast, Pop? *(Sits on hassock.)*

H.C. Let her sleep. She didn't sleep much last night.

JIM. Yeah. Gets off the train—comes home—and starts cleanin' up her bedroom in the middle of the night. Hell, there was no need for that. I cleaned her room up real nice.

H.C. *(Quietly)* Jimmy, when some girls ain't happy they cry— Lizzie works. *(Crosses Right Center; sits on chest.)*

JIM. Yeah. Well, what are we gonna do about her?

H.C. *(Worriedly)* I don't know.

JIM. We gotta do *somethin'*, Pop. We gotta at least talk to her. Mention!

H.C. Who's gonna mention it to her?

NOAH. I told you, Pop—I'm not gonna talk to her.

JIM. Me neither. I'm not gonna talk to her.

H.C. Stop sayin' exactly what Noah's sayin'. Speak for yourself.

JIM. I say what Noah is sayin' because I agree with him. When I don't, I spit in his eye.

H.C. Then why won't you talk to her?

JIM. Because if we do, she'll think we're tryin' to get rid of her.

H.C. She'll sure think the same if *I* do it.

NOAH. Maybe.

JIM. May *be.*

H.C. So there you are!

JIM. But you're her father and comes a time when a father's gotta mention.

H.C. I can't! I can't just speak up and say: "Lizzie, you gotta get married!" She knows she's gotta get married. We all know it.

NOAH. Well then—seems there's no point to mention anything.

(LIZZIE CURRY *comes down the stairs. At first glance, she seems a woman who can cope with all the aspects of her life. She has the world of materiality under control; she is a good housekeeper; pots and pans, needles and thread—when she touches them, they serve. She knows well where she fits in the family— she is daughter, sister, mother, child—and she enjoys the manifold elements of her position. She has a sure ownership of her own morality, for the tenets of right and wrong are friendly to her—and she is comfortably forthright in living by them. A strong and integral woman in every life function— except one. Here she is, twenty-seven years old, and no man outside the family has loved her or found her beautiful. And yet, ironically, it is this one unfulfilled part of* LIZZIE *that is the most potentially beautiful facet of the woman—this yearning for romance—this courageous searching for it in the desert of her existence— And if some day a man should find her, he will find a ready woman, willing to give herself with the totality of her rich being.)*

LIZZIE. Morning, Pop— *(Crosses to him.)* Noah— Jimmy. *(Runs around to gifts on floor Left Center; fixes belt.)*

H.C. Mornin', honey.

NOAH *and* JIM. Mornin', Lizzie— Hi, Liz.

LIZZIE. Sure good to be home again.

H.C. Just what the boys were sayin'—sure good to have Lizzie home again.

LIZZIE. No sign of rain yet, is there? *(To porch Right.)*

H.C. Not a cloud nowhere.

LIZZIE. I dreamed we had a rain—a great *big* rain!

H.C. Did you, Lizzie?

LIZZIE. Thunderstorm! Rain coming down in sheets! *(To Center.)* Lightning flashed—thunder rolled up and down the canyon like a kid with a big drum! I looked up and I laughed and yelled—! *(To door Right. With a laugh)* Oooh, it was wonderful!

NOAH. Drought's drought—and a dream's a dream.

LIZZIE. But it was a nice dream, Noah—and nearly as good as rain.

NOAH. Near ain't rain!

H.C. It's too bad we picked you up at the depot so late last night, Lizzie. Didn't have much time to talk about your trip.

NOAH. Looks like it perked you up real good. Yeah, you were lookin' all dragged out by the heat. What was it like in Sweetriver?

LIZZIE. *(To Left of table.)* Hotter'n hell.

(H.C. *and* JIM *laugh.*)

NOAH. I don't see nothin' funny in her talkin' like a cowhand.

LIZZIE. Sorry, Noah. That's about all the conversation I've heard for a week.

H.C. How's Uncle Ned, Lizzie? And Aunt Ivy.

JIM. And how's all them boys?

LIZZIE. Big.

H.C. If they take after Aunt Ivy I bet they talked your ear off.

LIZZIE. No, they take after Uncle Ned. They just grunt.

NOAH. Who got to be the best lookin' of the boys, Lizzie?

LIZZIE. Oh—I guess Pete. *(Left Center.)*

H.C. Never could get those boys straight. Which one is Pete?

LIZZIE. He's the one with the yellow hair.

NOAH. *(Quickly.)* Yella hair's nice in a man!

JIM. It's honest!

LIZZIE. Oh, Pete was honest all right.

JIM. The way you said that I bet you liked him the best.

LIZZIE. Oh, I'm crazy about Pete—he asked me to marry him.

(A moment.)

H.C. Is that true, Lizzie?

JIM. *(Agog.)* He did? ! What did you tell him? !

LIZZIE. I told him I would—as soon as he graduates from grammar school.

(Silence.)

JIM. Grammar school?! Is he that dumb?!

LIZZIE. *(With a laugh)* No. He's only nine years old. *(Seeing the stricken look on their faces, crosses down Left.)* Pop, let's not beat around the bush. I know why you sent me to Sweetriver.

(JIM *crosses to radio.)*

Because Uncle Ned's got six boys. Three of them are old enough to get married—and so am I. Well, I'm sorry you went to all that expense—the railroad ticket—all those new clothes—the trip didn't work. Noah, you can write it in the books—in red ink. *(At hassock.)*

H.C. *(Right Center on chest.)* What happened at Sweetriver, Lizzie?

LISSIE. *(Emptily)* Nothing— Not a doggone thing!

H.C. What did you do? Where'd you go?

LIZZIE. *(On floor Left Center, at suitcase.)* Well, the first three or four days I was there—I stayed in my room most of the time.

NOAH. What'd you do that for?

LIZZIE. Because I was embarrassed!

NOAH. Embarrassed about what?

LIZZIE. Noah, use your head! I knew what I was there for—and that whole family knew it too! And I couldn't stand the way they were looking me over. So I'd go downstairs for my meals—and rush right back to my room. I packed—I unpacked—I washed my hair a dozen times—I read the Sears, Roebuck catalog from

cover to cover! And finally I said to myself: "Lizzie
Curry, snap out of this!" Well, it was a Saturday night—
and they were all going to a rodeo dance. So I got
myself all decked out in my highest heels and my lowest
cut dress. And I walked down to that supper table and
all those boys looked at me as if I was stark naked. And
then for the longest while there wasn't a sound at the
table except for Uncle Ned slupping his soup. And then
suddenly—like a gunshot—I heard Ned Jr. say: "Lizzie,
how much do you weigh?"

H.C. What'd you say to that?

LIZZIE. *(Rises.)* I said, "I weigh a hundred and nine-
teen pounds, my teeth are all my own and I stand seven-
teen hands high."

NOAH. That wasn't very smart of you, Lizzie. He was
just tryin' to open the conversation.

LIZZIE. *(Wryly. Puts suitcase up Left.)* Well, I guess
I closed it.—Then, about ten minutes later Little Pete
came hurrying in to the supper table. He was carrying
a geography book and he said: "Hey, Pop—where's
Madagascar?" Well, everybody ventured an opinion and
they were all dead wrong. And suddenly I felt I had to
make a good impression and I said: "It's an island in
the Indian Ocean off the coast of Africa right opposite
Mozambique." *(With a wail)* Can I help it if I was
good in geography?

(JIM to door Right.)

H.C. What happened?

LIZZIE. Everything was so quiet it sounded like the
end of the world. Then I heard Ned Jr.'s voice: "Lizzie,
you fixin' to be a schoolmarm?"

H.C. Oh no.

LIZZIE. *(Sits hassock.)* Yes. And suddenly I felt like
I was way back at the high school dance—and nobody
dancing with me. And I had a sick feeling that I was
wearing eyeglasses again the way I used to. And I knew
from that minute on that it was no go! So I didn't go

to the rodeo dance with them—I stayed home and made up poems about what was on sale at Sears, Roebuck's.

H.C. You and little Pete?

LIZZIE. Yes— And the day I left Sweetriver little Pete was bawling. And he said: "You're the beautifulest girl that ever was!"

H.C. *(Crosses to her.)* And he's right! You are!

LIZZIE. *(More pain than pleasure)* Oh Pop, please—!

H.C. *We* see you that way—*he* saw you that way—

LIZZIE. But not his big brothers!

H.C. Because you didn't *show* yourself right!

LIZZIE. I tried, Pop—I tried!

H.C. No you didn't! You hid behind your books! You hid behind your glasses that you don't even wear no more! You're *afraid* of bein' beautiful!

LIZZIE. *(In an outburst. Rises; then to kitchen.)* I'm afraid to *think* I am when I *know* I'm *not!!*

(Her intensity stops the discussion. NOAH replaces ledgers on cupboard; then to Right Center.)

H.C. Lizzie—?

LIZZIE. *(Off Left.)* Yes?

H.C. *(Center.)* Me and the boys—we put our heads together—and we thought we'd mention somethin' to you.

LIZZIE. What?

(JIM at door Right.)

H.C. *(Uncomfortably, to NOAH)* You want to tell her about it, Noah?

NOAH. Nope. It's your idea, Pop.

H.C. Well, the boys and me—after we get some work done—we figure to ride into Three Point this afternoon.

LIZZIE. *(Enters; to Left of table.)* Well?

H.C. We're goin' to the Sheriff's office and gonna talk to his deputy.

LIZZIE. *(Alert now.)* File?

H.C. Yes— File.

LIZZIE. Pop, that's the craziest idea—

H.C. I'm just gonna invite him to supper, Lizzie!

LIZZIE. If you do, I won't be here!

H.C. I can invite a fella to supper in my own house, can't I?

LIZZIE. I don't want you to go out and lasso a husband for me!

H.C. I won't do anything of the kind! I won't even say your name! We'll start talkin' about · a poker game maybe—and then we'll get around to supper—and before you know it, he'll be sittin' right in that chair!

LIZZIE. No!

H.C. *(Gets hat on sofa, then crosses Right Center.)* Lizzie, we're goin'—no matter what you say!

NOAH. *(Right of H.C.)* Hold on, Pop. I'm against this. But if Lizzie says it's okay to go down there and talk to File—I'll go right along with you. But one thing! We won't do it if Lizzie says no!

LIZZIE. And that's what I say—no!

H.C. Don't listen to Noah! Every time you and Jim have to scratch your back, you turn and ask Noah!

LIZZIE. Because he's the only sensible one around here, Pop! The three of us—we get carried away and then—

H.C. *(Interrupting hotly)* For once in your life—*get* carried away!—it won't hurt you!—not a bit!

NOAH. That's the dumbest advice I ever heard!

H.C. What's so dumb about it?

NOAH. It's a matter of pride!

(As LIZZIE turns away, H.C. sees her rejection of "pride" as a reason for not going through with the plan. Now he confronts her with the question.)

H.C. Is that why you say no, Lizzie? *Pride?*

LIZZIE. *(Above sofa Avoiding the confrontation.)* Pop, if you want to invite somebody to supper—go ahead —but not File! He doesn't even know I'm on earth!

H.C. *(With a quiet smile)* He knows, Lizzie—he knows.

LIZZIE. No he doesn't! Whenever we ride into town, File's got a great big hello for you and Noah and Jim— but he's got nothing for me! He just barely sneaks his hat off his head—and that's all! He makes a *point* of ignoring me!

H.C. *(Quietly, crossing to her)* When a man makes a *point* of ignorin' you, he ain't ignorin' you at all.

(As she looks at him quickly.)

How about it, Lizzie? File for supper?

LIZZIE. *(In an outburst. Crosses around to Left Center.)* No— I don't like him!—no!—no!

H.C. If you don't really like him—one no is enough— And you can say it quiet.

LIZZIE. *(Controlling herself—quietly, deliberately)* All right—I don't like him. I don't like the way he tucks his thumbs in his belt—and I don't like the way he always seems to be thinking deep thoughts!

H.C. *(Secretly amused.)* I thought you liked people with deep thoughts.

LIZZIE. Not File! *(Crosses Left.)*

(JIM crosses to Center.)

H.C. *(Right of her. Gently—soberly)* Lizzie—when you were a kid—if I ever thought you were lyin'—I'd say to you: "Honest in truth?" And then you'd never lie. Well, I'm sayin' it now— You don't like File?—honest in truth?

LIZZIE. *(Flustered.)* Oh Pop—that's silly!

H.C. I asked you a question. Honest in truth?

LIZZIE. *(Chattering evasively.)* Pop, that's a silly childish game and all you'll get is a silly childish answer and I refuse—I simply refuse to—to—

(JIM, who has picked up belt, Left, throws it on floor. Exits Right.)

(But suddenly she puts the brakes on. In an outburst.) Oh, for God sake, go on and invite him!

H.C. *(With a whooping shout)* O-kaaay! Come on, boys! *(At the doorway.)* You go ahead and cook a great supper, Lizzie!

(The MEN *hurry out. For an instant,* LIZZIE *is unnerved, alarmed at what she has let herself in for. Then suddenly, her spirits rising with expectancy, she goes about clearing the breakfast dishes. When* LIZZIE *is happy she dances as she works.* LIZZIE *is dancing. The LIGHTS fade.)*

(The LIGHTS come up to disclose the inside of FILE'S *office. There is an ancient rolltop desk with an old style telephone on it. On the wall, a bulletin board with various "Wanted" posters featuring the faces of criminals. His bed is a well-worn leather couch in the corner of the office. The walls are warmly stained knotty pine. The office is empty a moment, then* FILE *enters, followed by* SHERIFF THOMAS. FILE'S *thumbs, as* LIZZIE *described them, are tucked in his belt. He is a lean man, reticent, intelligent, in his late thirties. He smiles wryly at the world and at himself. Perhaps he is a little bitter; if so, his bitterness is leavened by a mischievous humor. He and the* SHERIFF *are deep in argument. Actually, it is the* SHERIFF *who is arguing;* FILE *is detached, humoring the* SHERIFF'S *argument. The men are obviously fond of each other.)*

SHERIFF. File!—will you listen to me, File!

FILE. Look here, Sheriff. When I was dead broke, you lent me some money. When I needed a job, you made me your deputy. When I catch cold, you bring me a mustard plaster. And now you want to give me a dog! Well, I *don't want a dog!*

SHERIFF. I won't charge you nothin' for it, File.

FILE. You never charge me for anything! I *don't want a dog!*

SHERIFF. How do you know you don't want him until you see him?

FILE. Well—I seen dogs before.

SHERIFF. Not this one—he's different. I tell you, File —you see this little fella and you'll reach out and wanta hug him to death.

FILE. *(Humoring him)* Think I will, huh?

SHERIFF. Yes you will! He's real lovin'! If you're sittin' in your bare feet, he'll come over and lick your big toe. And pretty soon, there he is—dead asleep—right across your feet! How about it, File?

FILE. *(Hesitating.)* Well—that sounds real homey— but I'll do without him.

SHERIFF. File, you make me disgusted. It ain't right for you to shack up all by yourself—with a coffee pot and a leather sofa! Especially once you been married. When you lose your wife, the nights get damn cold. And you gotta have somethin' warm up against your backside!

FILE. Well, last night was a hundred and four degrees.

SHERIFF. All right—if you don't want the dog—if you're the kind of fella that don't like animals—

FILE. *(Amused.)* I like animals, Sheriff.

SHERIFF. If you liked animals, you'd *have* animals!

FILE. Oh, I've had 'em.

SHERIFF. *(Disbelievingly)* I'll bet! What kind?

FILE. Well, back in Pedleyville—I went out and got myself a raccoon.

SHERIFF. A raccoon ain't a dog!

FILE. *(With a smile)* No—I guess it ain't. But I liked him. He was a crazy little fella—made me laugh!

SHERIFF. Yeah?—Whatever happened to him?

FILE. I don't know. One day he took to the woods and never came back, the little bastard.

SHERIFF. *(Triumphantly)* There!—see? Now can you figure a *dog* doin' that?—no sir! I tell you, File, if you never had a dog—

FILE. Oh, I had a dog.

SHERIFF. *(Defensively)* When did you have a dog?

FILE. When I was a kid.

SHERIFF. *(Testing for the truth of it)* What kind of dog was it?

FILE. Mongrel. Just a kid's kind.

SHERIFF. What'd you call him?

FILE. Dog.

SHERIFF. No, I mean what was his name?

FILE. Dog!

SHERIFF. *(Exasperated.)* Didn't you have no name for him?

FILE. Dog!—that was his name—Dog!

SHERIFF. That ain't no fittin' name for a dog!

FILE. I don't see why not!

SHERIFF. *(Shocked.)* You don't see why not? !

FILE. Nope. He always came when I called him.

SHERIFF. *(Almost apoplectic.)* Hell, man, you couldn't of liked him much if you didn't even give him a name!

FILE. Oh, I liked him a lot, Sheriff. Gave him everything he wanted. Took good care of him too—better than he took care of himself.

SHERIFF. Why? What happened to *him?*

FILE. Dumb little mutt ran under a buckboard.

SHERIFF. Well, hell—you figure everythin's gonna run away—or get run over? !

FILE. *(With a smile)* Oh, I dunno— I just don't want a dog, Sheriff. Not that I ain't obliged.

SHERIFF. Stubborn as a mule— Well, I guess I'll have a look around—see what's doin'. *(Gets hat.)*

FILE. *(As the* SHERIFF *goes)* Yeah— Sleeps on your feet, does he?

SHERIFF. *(Laughing)* Right on my feet! Right on my big old stinkin' feet!—See you later, File. *(He goes out.)*

(When the SHERIFF *has gone,* FILE *discovers a rip in his shirt. He reaches into a drawer of his desk, pulls out a cigar box, opens it and extracts needle and thread. He has just begun to mend the tear when he hears the voices of the* CURRY MEN. *Lest they catch him in the un-mannish act of sewing, he puts*

the cigar box back and, forgetting the needle, lets it dangle from his shirt. The three CURRY MEN *enter. They are embarrassed about their errand, and, although they have plotted a plan of action, they're nervous about its outcome.* NOAH *is sullenly against this whole maneuver.)*

FILE. Hey, H.C. Hey, boys.

H.C., NOAH *and* JIM. Hey, File— Hey, File— Hey, File.

FILE. Ridin' over, you boys see any sign of rain?

NOAH. Not a spit.

FILE. *(With a trace of a smile, but not unkindly.)* What's it like in Sweetriver?

NOAH. *(Tensing a little)* How'd *we* know? We ain't been to Sweetriver.

FILE. Sheriff says that Lizzie's been to Sweetriver.

H.C. Yeah.

FILE. What's it like?

NOAH. Dry.

FILE. How'd Lizzie like it in Sweetriver?

NOAH. *(Sensing that their legs are being pulled)* Fine. —She liked it fine!

JIM. *(Readying for a fight)* Yeah—she liked it fine! Three barn dances, a rodeo, a summer fair and larkin' all over the place. *(He laughs loudly.)*

(NOAH *squirms as he realizes that* FILE *sees through them. And* H.C. *feels queasy. Then, jumping in:)*

H.C. How's your poker, File?

FILE. My what?

H.C. Poker.

FILE. Oh, I don't like poker much.

JIM. You don't?! Don't you like Spit in the Ocean?!

FILE. Not much.

H.C. We figured to ask you to play some cards.

FILE. I gave cards up a long time ago, H.C.

JIM. *(Stymied.)* You did, huh?
FILE. Mm-hm.

(Silence. An impasse. Suddenly JIM *sees the needle hanging down from* FILE'S *shirt.)*

JIM. File, what's that hangin' down from your shirt?
FILE. *(A little self-consciously)* Kinda looks like a needle.
H.C. It sure does.
JIM. What's the matter—your shirt tore?
FILE. Looks like it.
JIM. Fix it yourself, do you?
FILE. Sure do.
JIM. *(Clucking in sympathy)* Tch-tch-tch-tch-tch-tch.
FILE. *(Suppressing the smile)* Oh, I wouldn't say that, Jim. I been fixin' my own shirts ever since I became a widower back in Pedleyville.
JIM. Lizzie fixes all my shirts.
FILE. Well, it sure is nice to have a sister.
JIM. *(Significantly)* Or *somethin'!*

(Silence. An impasse.)

FILE. Did—uh—did Lizzie come back from Sweetriver by herself?
NOAH. *(Tensing)* Sure! She *went* by herself, didn't she?
FILE. *(With a dry smile)* That don't mean nothin'. I rode down to Leverstown to buy myself a mare. I *went* by myself but I came *back* with a mare!
JIM. *(Getting the point; starting to lose his temper.)* Well, she didn't go to buy nothin'! Get it, File—nothin'!
FILE. *(Evenly.)* Don't get ornery, Jim. I just asked a friendly question.
NOAH. *(To* JIM—*with hidden warning)* Sure! Just a friendly question—don't get ornery.
H.C. *(Baiting the trap for* FILE) I always say to Jim

—the reason you ain't got no *real* friends is 'cause you're ornery! You just don't know how to make friends!

JIM *(Hurt and angry.)* Sure I do—sure I do!

H.C. No you don't! *(Meaningfully)* Do you ever ask a fella out to have a drink?—no! Do you ever say to a fella: Come on home and have some supper?!

JIM. *(Suddenly remembering the objective; not sure how to spring the trap.)* I guess you're right. I'm sorry, File. Didn't mean to get ornery. Come on out and have a drink.

NOAH. *(Reflexively) Supper!*

JIM. *(Quickly, realizing his error)* Yeah—come on home and have some supper.

FILE. *(Aware of the trap.)* Guess I'll say no to the supper, boys. *(With a flash of mischief)* But I'll be glad to go out and have a drink with you.

NOAH. We don't have time for a drink. But we been figurin' to ask you to supper one of these days.

FILE. Be glad to come—one of these days.

H.C. How about tonight?

FILE. Don't have the time tonight. Seems there's some kind of outlaw comin' this way. Fella named Tornado Johnson. Have to stick around.

NOAH. You don't know he'll come *this* way, do you?

FILE. They say he's Three Point bound.

H.C. But you don't know he'll be here *tonight.*

FILE. I don't know he *won't* be here tonight.

JIM. Why he might be down at Pedleyville or Peak's Junction. He might even be over at our place.

FILE. *(Quietly)* Well, *I* won't be over at your place, Jim.

JIM. *(Riled—to H.C.)* You said for me to be friendly! Well, I'm tryin' but he don't *want* to be friendly!

FILE. *(Evenly.)* I want to be friendly, Jim—but I don't want to be married.

(A flash of tense silence.)

JIM. *(Exploding)* Who says we're invitin' you over for Lizzie?! You take that back!

FILE. Won't take nothin' back, Jim!
JIM. Then take somethin' else!

(JIM's *fist flashes out but* FILE *is too quick for him. He parries the single blow and levels off one of his own. It connects squarely with* JIM's *eye and* JIM *goes down. The fight is over that quickly.*)

NOAH. *(Tensely, to* FILE.) If I didn't think he had it comin', I'd wipe you up good and clean!
FILE. He had it comin'.

(An instant. NOAH *is the most humiliated of all of them.*)

NOAH. *(To* H.C. *more than to* FILE.) I guess we all did. *(To* JIM.) Come on, turtlehead, let's go home.

(NOAH *goes out quickly, followed by* JIM. *But* H.C. *remains with* FILE. *Silence.* FILE *speaks quietly.*)

FILE. I shouldn't of hit him, H.C.
H.C. Oh that's all right. Only thing is—you know you lost that fight.
FILE. What?
H.C. Yeah. It wouldn't of hurt you to come to supper. It mighta done you some good.
FILE. We weren't talkin' about supper!
H.C. *(Meeting the confrontation squarely.)* That's right. We were talkin' about Lizzie. And she mighta done you some good too.
FILE. I can mend my own shirts.
H.C. Seems to me you need a lot more mendin' than shirts. (H.C. *starts for the door.*)
FILE. Wait a minute, H.C.! You don't drop a word like that and just leave it!
H.C. All right—what'd you hit him for?
FILE. He threw a punch! I got angry!
H.C. Angry?—why? We come around here and say

we like you enough to have you in our family. Is that an insult?

FILE I don't like people interferin'.

H.C. Interferin' with what?!

FILE. I'm doin' all right—by myself!

H.C. You ain't doin' all right! A fella who won't make friends with a whole town that likes him and looks up to him—a fella who locks himself in—he ain't doin' all right! And if he says he is, he's a liar!

FILE. Take it easy, H.C.!

H.C. I said a liar and I mean it! You talk about yourself as bein' a widower! We all got respect for your feelin's—but you ain't a widower—and everybody in this town knows it!

FILE. *(Losing his temper)* I am a widower! My wife died six years ago—back in Pedleyville!

H.C. Your wife didn't die, File--she ran out on you! And you're a divorced man! But we'll all go on calling you a widower as long as you want us to! Hell, it don't hurt *us* none— But you—! A fella who shuts himself up with that lie—he needs mendin'! *(A moment.)* Want to throw any more punches?

(FILE *slowly turns away from him. H.C. goes out. Brooding,* FILE *goes back to his desk. He resumes the mending of his shirt but his mind is not on it: his thoughts are turned inward. The LIGHTS fade.)*

(*The LIGHTS come up on the Curry house again.* LIZZIE *is just finishing the supper preparations. She works competently, quickly, bubbling with excitement. A quick survey of the kitchen—everything is fine. Now she has to dress. She hurries to the dining room and notices there are only four chairs around the table. She shoves two chairs apart, gets another one and pushes it up against the table to make the fifth. The sight of five chairs instead of the customary four is exhilarating to her. Singing, she hurries toward the stairs. At this moment,* NOAH *comes in.*

He is in low, disgruntled spirits—but seeing LIZZIE, *he tries to smile.)*

LIZZIE. You all back so soon? *(Chattering excitedly)* Now don't walk heavy because the lemon cake will fall! You told File six o'clock, I hope!

NOAH. Uh—we didn't tell him no exact time.

LIZZIE. *(In a spate of words)* Now that's real smart! Suppose he comes at seven and all the cooking goes dry! I got the prettiest lemon cake in the oven—and a steak and kidney pie as big as that table! Oh, look at me— I better change my dress or I'll get caught looking a mess! *(As she starts up the stairs he tries to stop her.)*

NOAH. Lizzie—

(Just then the PHONE rings.)

LIZZIE. Answer the telephone, will you, Noah? And don't let Jimmy near the table. He'll mess it up. (LIZZIE *rushes upstairs.)*

(The PHONE rings again and NOAH *answers it.)*

NOAH. Hello.

(JIM *enters Right. He has an effulgent black eye.)* *(Into phone—annoyed at the instrument.)* Hello—hello! No, this ain't Jim—it's Noah. Who's this? *(To* JIM— *darkly)* It's Snookie Maguire.

JIM. Hot dog!

(He catapults across the room and reaches for receiver. But NOAH, *with one hand over the mouthpiece, withholds the receiver from* JIM *with his other hand.)*

NOAH. What exactly do you mean—hot dog?

JIM. *(Lamely)* Just hot dog, Noah.

NOAH. What are you gonna say to her?

JIM. I don't know what *she's* gonna say to *me!*

NOAH. *(Handing phone)* Well, watch out.

JIM. *(Into phone—he coos lovingly.)* Hello— Hello, Snookie— Oh I'm fine— I'm just fine and dandy! How are *you!* Fine and dandy? Well, I'm sure glad you're fine and dandy too!

NOAH. *(Muttering disgustedly)* Fine-and-dandy-my-big-foot!

JIM. *(So sweetly)* I was gonna telephone *you,* Snookie. But you telephoned *me,* di'n't you? Ain't that the prettiest coincidence?

NOAH. *(Nauseated.)* Jimmy, for Pete sake!

JIM. *(Into phone.)* What?—You mean it, Snookie? You mean it? Gee, I sure hope you mean it!

NOAH. What's all that you mean it about?

JIM. *(To NOAH—in raptures.)* She says: "It's a hot night and the Essex is sayin' 'Chug-chug, where's little Jimmy?' "

NOAH. Well, you tell her chug-chug, little Jimmy's gonna sit home on his little fat bottom!

JIM. Now wait a minute, Noah—!

NOAH. Don't say wait a minute! If you wanta get mixed up with poison, you go right ahead! But I wash my hands!

JIM. *(Unhappily—into phone)* Hello, Snookie— I just can't tonight— *(Confused.)* Well, I don't *know* why exactly. Anyway, I can't talk now— Oh, Snookie— *(Longingly)* —are you still wearin' your little red hat? *(Relieved.)* That's fine, Snookie—you take care of that! —Goodbye, Snookie. *(He hangs up.)*

NOAH. See that?—You go out with her once and she starts chasin' you!

JIM. Well, I don't see what's wrong with that, Noah.

NOAH. *(Shocked.)* You don't?!

JIM. No! People want to get together—they oughta get together. It don't matter how, does it?

NOAH. *(Gets ledger from cupboard.)* Now you ask yourself if it don't really matter.—Go on and ask yourself, Jimmy! *(Sits Right Center chest with ledger.)*

JIM. *(Suddenly lost when he has to figure it out for*

himself. Up to radio.) Well, maybe it does— Holy
mackerel, I sure wish I could figure things out. If only
I could get somethin' on this crystal set—somethin'!
You think I could get Kansas City on this thing?

NOAH. Nope!

JIM. Yeah?—Well maybe I got it and I didn't know
it! The other day I fiddled with this set and suddenly I
hear a sound like the prettiest music! And I says to
myself: "Sonofagun, I got Kansas City!"

NOAH. Static—that's all—just static!

JIM. I knew you'd say that, Noah. And I figured the
answer to it: If it *feels* like Kansas City, it *is* Kansas
City!

NOAH. Then why don't you make it feel like Africa?

JIM. On this little crystal set?

H.C. *(Comes in Right; to above* NOAH.) **Where's**
Lizzie? Did you tell her?

NOAH. No—she ran upstairs to get dressed.

(LIZZIE *comes hurrying down the stairs. She is all
dressed up and in a flurry of anticipation.)*

LIZZIE. *(Crosses Center.)* Well, folks, how do I look?

H.C. *(To Center.)* Beautiful!

JIM. Great—beautiful!

LIZZIE. You know, Pop—I really think I am!—if you
don't look too close! *(Exuberantly.)* When do you suppose File will get here? I ought to know *some* time we
can start eating!

H.C. *(Quietly; sits on sofa.)* We can start any time
you say.

LIZZIE. Any time? *(She looks at him quickly—and
quickly gets the point. Then, pretending that life goes
on unchanged, even trying to see some advantage in*
FILE'S *not coming, she rattles on with studied casualness.)* Well, you better wash up—and we can have more
room at the table and— *(She has gone to the table to
remove* FILE'S *fifth chair, but she cannot bring herself
to do it.)* —File's not coming—

H.C. No.

LIZZIE. *(Right, at door.)* I see.

JIM. *(Quickly.)* Not that he didn't want to come! He wanted to—a lot! *(To Left at kitchen.)*

LIZZIE. He did, huh?

JIM. Sure! Pop said: "Come to supper tonight, File." And when Pop said that— *(Quickly, to H.C.)* —did you notice how his face kinda—well—it lighted up? Did you notice that?

H.C. *(Lamely.)* Yeah.

JIM. And then File said: "Sure—sure I'll come! Glad to come!" And then suddenly he remembered.

LIZZIE. *(Quietly—not at all taken in.)* What did he remember, Jimmy?

JIM. *(Crossing Right)* Well, he remembered there's some kind of outlaw runnin' around. And he better stick around and pay attention to his job. Business before pleasure! *(Sits on chest beside NOAH. Pleased with himself.)* Yessir, File was real friendly!

LIZZIE. Friendly, huh? What happened to your eye? *(Pulls him to Center.)*

JIM. It kinda swole up on me.

NOAH. File hit him.

LIZZIE. You mean you fought to get him to come here?

JIM. It was only a *little* fight, Lizzie.

LIZZIE. *(Trying to laugh.)* Why didn't you make it a big one—a riot! Why didn't you all just pile on and slug him!

JIM. *(Sits in chair Left of table.)* Lizzie, you're seein' this all wrong.

LIZZIE. I'm seeing it the way it happened! He said: "She might be a pretty good cook—and it might be a good supper—but she's plain! She's as plain as old shoes!"

H.C. He didn't say anything like that!

JIM. He didn't say nothin' about shoes!

H.C. Lizzie—we made a mess out of it.

NOAH. If you'da taken my advice there wouldn't of been a mess! I said don't go down and talk to File—

nobody listened. I said don't send her to Sweetriver—
nobody listened! Hell, I don't like to be right all the
time! But for God's sake—!

H.C. *(To above Center.)* Well, Noah, I'm stumped.
If you were Lizzie's father, what would you do?

NOAH. *(To Right of table.)* Who says we gotta do
anything? We been pushin' her around—tryin' to marry
her off! Why? What if she don't get married? Is that
the end of everything?! She's got a home! She's got a
family—she's got bed and board and clothes on her
back and plenty to eat!

LIZZIE. *(Left of* JIM.) That's right. From now on we
listen to Noah!

H.C. No! Don't you dare listen to him!

NOAH. *(Sits Right of table.)* Why not? She's got
everything she needs!

H.C. She ain't got what'll make her happy!

JIM. And she ain't gonna get it!

(As they ALL *look at him in surprise.)*
Because she's goin' at it all wrong!

LIZZIE. How, Jimmy? How am I going at it wrong?

JIM. Because you don't talk to a man the way you
oughta! You talk too serious! And if there's anything
scares hell out of a fella it's a serious-talkin' girl!

H.C. *(Above table Center.)* Well, that's the way Lizzie
is!—and she can't be anything else!

JIM. Yes she can! She's as smart as any of them girls
down at the Ladies' Social Club! She can go down to
the Social on Wednesday nights—and she can giggle
and flirt as good as any of them!

(LIZZIE crosses to sofa and sits.)

H.C. What do you want her to turn into—Lily Ann
Beasley?!

JIM. Lily Ann Beasley gets any man she goes for! Why,
I saw her walk up to Phil Mackie one mornin'—and she
wiggled her hips like a cocker spaniel and she said: "Phil
Mackie, how many toes have you got?" And he said,

"Well, naturally—I got ten." And she said, "Why, that's just the right number of toes for a big strong man to have!" And pretty soon he was cooked! He started followin' her around—and she got him so nervous, he bust right out with the shingles!

LIZZIE. Well, if she wants Phil Mackie she can have him!—shingles and all!

JIM. And how about that livestock fella from Chicago—?!

LIZZIE. Jimmy!—can I treat a man the way she treated him?! *(Imitating Lily Ann)* "My—a polka dot tie! I just adore a man with a polka dot tie! Those little round dots go right to my heart!"

JIM. Yeah—and that poor fella—the blood rushed out of his face and I thought he'd keel right over in the horse trough!

LIZZIE. *(Crosses to kitchen.)* I don't *want* a man to keel over! I want him to stand up straight—and I want to stand up straight *to* him! Without having to trick him! *(With a cry)* Isn't that possible with a man?!—isn't it *possible?!*

NOAH. No, it ain't!

H.C. Yes it is, Lizzie!

NOAH. No! For once in his life, Jim said somethin' sensible. *(Confronting* LIZZIE *quietly)* If it's a man you want, you gotta get him *the way a man gets got!*

LIZZIE If that's the way a man gets got, I don't want any of them!

H.C. Lizzie—

LIZZIE. No! To hell with File! To hell with all of them!

NOAH. Don't use that language!

LIZZIE. Hell—hell—hell! To hell with all of them!

(It is an outcry straight from the heart—rebellious but aching—and they can do nothing to help her. Suddenly, the outside door swings open, screaming on its hinges, whacking the wall like a pistol shot. EVERYBODY *turns to the door, but all they can see is a vista of sky—no one is there. But we, in the*

audience, see BILL STARBUCK *just outside the door.
He is a big man, lithe, agile—a loud braggart, a
gentle dreamer. He carries a short hickory stick—
it is his weapon, his pointer, his magic wand, his
pride of manhood.)*

NOAH　Who opened that door?

(LIZZIE *rises; to stairs Left.)*

JIM. Musta been the wind!

STARBUCK. *(Steps onto the threshold. He hears* JIM'S
line about the wind.) Wind?—did you say wind? There's
not a breath of wind anywhere in the world!

NOAH. Who are *you?*

STARBUCK. The name's Starbuck! Starbuck is the
name! *(He espies* LIZZIE *and his whole manner changes.
He doffs his hat and his bow is part gallantry, part
irony. Crosses to her.)* Lady of the house—*hello!*

LIZZIE. *(Involuntarily)* Hello.

STARBUCK. That's a mighty nice dress—it oughta go
to a party!

LIZZIE. *(Not charmed.)* Don't you knock on a door
before you come in?

H.C. *(Right Center.)* What is it? What can we do for
you?

STARBUCK. *(Left Center.)* You're askin' the wrong
question. The question is what can I do for you?

NOAH. I don't remember we called for anybody to do
anything.

STARBUCK. You should have, Mister—you sure should
have! You need a lot of help! You're in a parcel of
trouble. You lost twelve steers on the north range and
sixty-two in the gully. The calves are starvin' and the
heifers are down on their knees.

JIM. *(Up Right Cnter.)* You know a heckuva lot about
our herd!

STARBUCK. *(Noticing* JIM'S *black eye)* Man, that sure
is a shiner! *(To* H.C.) Your ranch, Mister?

NOAH. He owns it—I run it.

STARBUCK. *(To* NOAH.*)* Well, I guess I'll talk to *you.* You got a look of business about you, Mister. You got your feet apart—and you stand solid on the ground! That's the kind of a man I like to talk to! Well, what are you gonna do about them cattle?

NOAH. If you know we lost the cattle, you oughta know what killed them. Drought! Ever hear of it?

STARBUCK. Hear of it! That's *all* I hear! Wherever I go, there's drought ahead of me! But when I leave— behind me there's rain—*rain!*

LIZZIE. *(On step Left.)* I think this man's crazy!

STARBUCK. *(Crosses down Left.)* Sure!—that's what I am!—crazy! I woke up this mornin'—I looked at the world and I said to myself: "The world's gone completely out of its mind! And the only thing that can set it straight is a first class, A-number-one lunatic! Well, here I am, folks—crazy as a bedbug! Did I introduce myself? The name is Starbuck—*Rainmaker!*

H.C. *(Doubtfully)* I've heard about rainmakers. *(Offers Center chair, then lights lamp above sofa.)*

NOAH. I read about a rainmaker—I think it was Idaho.

STARBUCK. What'd you read, Mister?

NOAH. I can't remember whether they locked him up or ran him out of town.

STARBUCK. *(Sits Center chair. Laughing goodnatured-ly)* Might be they strung him up on a sycamore tree.

NOAH. *(Sits Right of table.)* Look, fella, the idea is— we don't believe in rainmakers.

STARBUCK. What *do* you believe in, Mister—dyin' cattle?

JIM. You really mean you can bring rain?

LIZZIE. He talks too fast—he can't bring anything!

JIM. *(Sits on hassock.)* I asked *him.* Can you bring rain?

STARBUCK. It's been done, brother—it's been done!

JIM. *(Excitedly)* Where? How?

(LIZZIE lights hanging lamp up Center.)

STARBUCK. *(Rises. With a flourish of his stick)* How? Sodium chloride!—pitch it up high—right up to the clouds! Electrify the cold front! Neutralize the warm front! Barometricize the tropopause! Magnetize occlusions in the sky! *(Crosses Right to door.)*

LIZZIE. *(Confronting him quietly.)* In other words—bunk!

STARBUCK. *(Realizing he will have to contend with* LIZZIE *and* NOAH, *he suddenly and shrewdly reverses his field—he agrees with her.)* Lady, you're right! You know why that sounds like bunk? Because it is bunk! Bunk and hokey pokey! And I tell you, I'd be ashamed to use any of those methods!

JIM. What method do you use?

STARBUCK. *(To up Left Center.)* My method's like my name—it's all my own! You want to hear my deal?

LIZZIE. We're not interested.

NOAH. Not one bit!

H.C. *(Crosses Center.)* What is it?

NOAH. Pop, you're not listenin' to this man—?!

H.C. *(Crosses to* STARBUCK. *Quietly)* Any charge for listenin'?

STARBUCK. No charge—free!

H.C. *(Crosses; sits on chest Right Center.)* Go ahead. What's the deal?

STARBUCK. *(Center.)* One hundred dollars in advance —and inside of twenty-four hours you'll have rain!

JIM. *(In a dither)* You mean it? Real rain?

STARBUCK. Rain is rain, brother! It comes from the sky! It's a wetness known as water! Aqua pura! Mammals drink it, fish swim in it, little boys wade in it, and birds flap their wings and sing like sunrise! Water! *(Left Center; pours water from pitcher over his head.)* I recommend it!

JIM. *(Convinced, crosses to* NOAH.) Pay him the hundred, Noah!

LIZZIE. *(Up Left Center.)* Noah, don't be a chump!

NOAH. Me?—don't worry—I won't!

JIM. We got the drought, Noah! It's rain, Lizzie—we need it!

LIZZIE. We won't get a drop of it!—not from him!

H.C. *(Quietly)* How would you do it, Starbuck?

STARBUCK. Now don't ask me no questions.

LIZZIE. Why? It's a fair question! How will you do it?

STARBUCK. *(Left Center.)* What do you care how I do it, sister, as long as it's done! But I'll tell you how I'll do it! I'll lift this stick and take a long swipe at the sky and let down a shower of hailstones as big as canteloupes! I'll shout out some good old Nebraska cusswords and you turn around and there's a lake where your corral used to be! Or I'll just sing a little tune maybe and it'll sound so pretty and sound so sad you'll weep and your old man will weep and the sky will get all misty-like and shed the prettiest tears you ever did see! How'll I do it?! Girl, I'll just do it!

NOAH. Where'd you ever bring rain before?

LIZZIE. What town? What state?

STARBUCK. Sister, the last place I brought rain is now called Starbuck—they named it after me! Dry? I tell you, those people didn't have enough damp to blink their eyes! So I get out my big wheel and my rolling drum and my yella hat with the three little feathers in it! I look up at the sky and I say: "Cumulus!" I say: "Cumulo-nimbus! Nimbulo-cumulus!" And pretty soon —way up there—there's a teeny little cloud the size of a mare's tail—and then over there—there's another cloud lookin' like a white-washed chicken house! And then I look up and all of a sudden there's a herd of white buffalo stampedin' across the sky! And then, sister-of-all-good-people, down comes the rain! *(Crosses to door Right.)* Rain in buckets, rain in barrels, fillin' the lowlands, floodin' the gullies! And the land is as green as the valley of Adam! And when I rode out of there I looked behind me and I see the prettiest colors in the sky—green, blue, purple, gold—colors to make you cry!

And me?! I'm ridin' right through that rainbow!—Well, how about it? Is it a deal? *(To Center.)*

H.C. Well—

LIZZIE. *(Seeing her father's indecision)* Pop—no! He's a liar and a con man!

H.C. *(Reluctantly)* Yep, that's what he is all right—**a liar and a con man!**

STARBUCK. *(Gets hat.)* Hurts me to hear you say that, Mister! Well, so long to you—so long for a sorry night! *(He starts for the door.)*

H.C. Wait a minute!

STARBUCK. *(Right Center.)* You said I was a con man!

H.C. *(To Left of him.)* You're a liar and a con man—but I didn't say I wouldn't take your deal!

LIZZIE. Pop—

H.C. *(Quickly, to LIZZIE)* I didn't say I *would*, neither!

NOAH. Pop, you ain't gonna throw away a hundred bucks! How do I write it in the books?!

H.C. Write it as a gamble, Noah! I've lost more'n that in poker on a Saturday night!

LIZZIE. *(Sits on sofa.)* You get an even chance in poker!

H.C. Lizzie, I knew an old fella once—and he had the asthma. He went to every doctor and still he coughed and still he wheezed. Then one day a liar and a con man come along and took the old man for fifty dollars and a gold-plated watch! But a funny thing——! After that con man left, the old boy never coughed one minute until the day he was kicked in the head by a horse!

LIZZIE. That's a crazy reason!

STARBUCK. I'll give you better reasons, Lizzie-girl! *(Crosses Left Center.)* You gotta take my deal because once in your life you gotta take a chance on a con man! You gotta take my deal because there's dyin' calves that might pick up and live! Because a hundred bucks is only a hundred bucks—but rain in a dry season is a sight to behold! You gotta take my deal because it's gonna be a hot night—and the world goes crazy on a hot night—and maybe that's what a hot night is for!

H.C. *(Right Center.)* Starbuck, you got you a deal!

STARBUCK. *(With a sudden smile)* Tell you: I knew I had a deal the minute I walked into this house!

JIM. How'd you know that?

STARBUCK. I see *four* of you and *five* places set for supper! And I says to myself: "Starbuck, your name's written right on that chair!" *(Picks up Center chair.)*

H.C. *(With a laugh)* Let's eat!

(STARBUCK *tosses his hat up on the rack, lifts up the chair, sets it back at its place by the table—and he is the first to sit! As the* OTHERS *sit down to supper—)*

END OF ACT ONE.

ACT TWO

SCENE: *Inside the Curry house, a short while after supper.* NOAH *is paying* STARBUCK *his fee, counting out the money on the dining table.* H.C. *is watching quietly;* JIM, *with keyed-up excitement.* LIZZIE *is clearing the supper dishes, hostile to the whole situation.*

NOAH. *(Standing Right of table, fuming as he counts out the bills.)* Seventy—eighty—eighty-five! I'm against this, Pop!

H.C. *(Seated above table, quietly)* Keep countin', Noah.

NOAH. Ninety—ninety-five—one hundred. There's your hundred bucks.

STARBUCK. *(Below table.)* Thank you, Noah.

(LIZZIE, *clearing table, takes tablecloth to porch; shakes it, pushing* STARBUCK *out of the way.)*

NOAH. Don't thank me—thank him! *(Going to his ledger on cupboard)* I'm writin' that down in my book! One hundred dollars—thrown away! *(Brings ledger to table, writes.)*

STARBUCK. *(Rises; to door Right.)* No—don't write that, Noah! Write it like this. Say: "On August the twenty-seventh, a man come stompin' through our doorway! We bid him time of night, we fed him a supper fit for a king and we gave him one hundred honest notes on the fair government of the United States of America! And in return for that hospitality he did us one small favor—he brought rain!" *(With a smile)* You got that? —Write it!

NOAH. I don't see no rain *yet!*

STARBUCK. *(To Center.)* I still got twenty-three hours to bring it!

NOAH. Well, you better get busy!

JIM. *(On sofa. Eagerly)* Yeah, Starbuck, you better knuckle down.

(STARBUCK *crosses to Center chair.* LIZZIE *takes it from under him.)*

STARBUCK. Now let's not get nervous! Rain, my friends, rain comes to the man that ain't nervous! *(Getting down to work. Sits beside* JIM *on sofa.)* Now—what kind of rain would you like?

JIM. You mean we can choose our kind?

(LIZZIE *gets book on phone table Left, then sits on chest Right Center.)*

STARBUCK. Sure you can choose your kind! And brother, there's all kinds! There's mizzle and there's drizzle—but you wouldn't want that! I generally give that away as a free sample! There's trickle and there's sprinkle! But that's for the little flower gardens of little pink old ladies. There's April showers that I can bring in April—but I can sometimes bring 'em in May. There's rain with thunder and rain with hail! There's flash floods—and storms that roll down the shoulder of the mountain! But the biggest of all—that's deluge! *(Modestly)* But don't ask me for deluge—that takes a bit of doin'!

JIM. What kind do we get for a hundred bucks?

STARBUCK. You choose it and I'll bring it!

LIZZIE. He brags so loud he gives me a pain in the neck!

STARBUCK. *(Rises; to Left Center.)* Look, folks, if you all act like she does, it's gonna make it mighty tough for me to do my job! Because when there's suspicion around, it's a *d-r-y* season!

(JIM crosses to him.)

LIZZIE. I don't doubt it. *(To sofa; sits.)*

STARBUCK. Well, she don't believe in me. How about the rest of you?

NOAH. What do you mean believe in you? We certainly don't!

STARBUCK. Then I changed my mind! I don't want your money—take it back! *(In a temper he slams the money on the table.)*

(They are stunned.)

H.C. Noah—please. We made a bargain—it's settled. Now be a good sport!

NOAH. *(Exasperated.)* Good sport?! What's he expect me to say?!

STARBUCK. I'll explain it to you, Noah. Makin' rain—it takes a lot of confidence! And if you have doubts about me—I get doubts about myself!

NOAH. Oh I see! If you don't bring rain, you're gonna blame it on us! We didn't have confidence! Well, we don't!

LIZZIE. You can steal our money—but that's *all* you can steal!

STARBUCK. *(In a temper)* That's not the right attitude!

JIM. *(Manfully)* I got the right attitude—take back your dough!

STARBUCK. No! What if I need some help?

JIM. I'll help you—so will Pop!

STARBUCK. But not him!

NOAH. *(To STARBUCK.)* What kind of help?

STARBUCK. *(To above sofa.)* Nothin' you can't do. How about you, lady? Any confidence?

LIZZIE. No confidence.

JIM. *(To Right of him.)* We don't need her, Starbuck—here's your dough. *(As STARBUCK takes it)* Now—what's the first step?

STARBUCK. *(Crosses around Left end of sofa to Center.)*

Well, what I'm gonna ask you to do—it ain't gonna make sense! But what's sensible about a flood or a hurricane?

JIM. Nothin'!

STARBUCK. Right! Now—what I want you to do: *(He hurries to the window Right and points out.)* You see that little old wagon of mine? On that wagon I got me a big bass drum. Somebody's gotta *beat* that drum!

NOAH. Beat it? What for?

(JIM *crosses to chest Right Center.)*

STARBUCK. Don't ask questions!

JIM. *(He has caught on to the rules of the game.)* And don't get sensible!

STARBUCK. That's right, Jimmy! Who's gonna beat that drum?

JIM. *(The stalwart.)* Me—I'll beat it!

STARBUCK. Jim, you're gonna be my first lieutenant! Now you go on out there and every time you get the feelin' for it, you beat that drum—three times—boom—boom—boom—low, like thunder— Got it?

JIM. Got it! Every time I get the feelin'?

STARBUCK. That's it.

JIM. *(Eagerly)* When do I start?

STARBUCK. Mister, you've started!

(JIM *goes out Right quickly.)*

(STARBUCK *to Left of table and sits.)* Mister H.C., I want you to pay close attention. In that wagon I got a bucket of white paint! Now it ain't ordinary white paint —it's special!—it's electro-magnetized, oxygenated, *de*-chromated white! Now I want you to go out there and paint a great big white arrow pointin' away from the house. That's so the house don't get struck by lightnin'!

H.C. *(To door Right; with a wry smile)* That sounds reasonable.

STARBUCK. *(Pretending to talk to himself, but his eye on* NOAH.) Now—it's too bad you ain't got a mule on the place.

NOAH. *(Muttering)* We got a mule.

STARBUCK. You have? That's great—that's just dandy! Noah, get a length of strong rope and go out there and tie that mule's hind legs together!

NOAH. What?! Tie the hind legs of a mule?!! What the hell for?!

STARBUCK. *(Hurt.)* Please—now, please—you gotta do like I *ask* you!

NOAH. I ain't gonna do it!

H.C. *(Crosses to* NOAH; *leads him to Right door.)* Come on, Noah!

NOAH. I'll be damned!—tie the hind legs of a mule!

(In a huff, NOAH *hurries outdoors.* H.C. *starts to follow him when* LIZZIE's *voice stops him.)*

LIZZIE. *(Rises; to Center.)* Pop—wait! *(As* H.C. *stops, she turns to him, livid with rage.)* Pop—I'm ashamed of you! I've been standing here—keeping my mouth shut—wondering how far you'd let this man go in making a fool of you!

H.C. *(Quietly)* He can't make me any more fool than I make out of myself.

LIZZIE. Where's your common sense?! Hang on to a little of it!

H.C. You mean go along with this fella halfway, huh? Well, I can't do that. I gotta take a chance on him—the whole chance—without fear of gettin' hurt or gettin' cheated or gettin' laughed at— As far as he'll take me. *(To* STARBUCK—*confronting him levelly.)* A white arrow, did you say?

STARBUCK. *(A moment. Then, meeting his glance, his response to* H.C. *is serious, even respectful.)* A white arrow, H.C.

H.C. *(Crosses to door.)* I'll paint it.

STARBUCK. *(Right Center. With the faintest touch of desperation)* Dammit, Mister, you're gonna get your money's worth if it's the last thing I do!

H.C. *(With a quiet smile—gently)* Don't get nervous, Boy.

STARBUCK. I ain't—not a bit of it!

H.C. That's fine. Confidence!

(H.C. *goes out. From outdoors, we hear the first deep, pompous sound of the BASS DRUM—boom—boom boom.)*

STARBUCK. *(Calling to* JIM) Attaboy, Jim—you beat that drum! Make it rumble!

JIM'S VOICE. *(In the spirit of things)* Make it rum-bullll! encourge

(The DRUM sounds off again.)

LIZZIE. *(Left Center, fuming with anger, whirls on* STARBUCK.) Well! I'll bet you feel real proud of your-self! mock

STARBUCK. *(Smiling evenly)* Kinda proud, sure. Terse

LIZZIE. *(Raging)* You're not satisfied to steal our money! You have to make jackasses out of us! Why'd you send them out on those fool errands! Why? What for?!

STARBUCK. *(Right Center.)* Maybe I thought it was necessary.

LIZZIE. *(Sits Center chair.)* You know good and well it wasn't necessary— *(Kicks* STARBUCK's *stick off hassock.)* You know it!

STARBUCK. Maybe I sent them out so's I could talk to you alone!

LIZZIE. *(Her rage mounting)* Then why didn't you just say it straight out: Lizzie, I want to talk to you—alone! —man to man!

STARBUCK. *(Quietly)* Man to man, Lizzie?

LIZZIE. *(Bitingly)* Excuse me—I made a mistake—you're not a man! *(Fusses with buttons on her dress.)*

STARBUCK. *(Tenses, then controls his anger.)* Lizzie, can I ask you a little question?

LIZZIE. No!

STARBUCK. I'll ask it anyway. Why are you fussin' at the buttons on your dress?

LIZZIE. Fussing at the—! I'm not! *(And she stops doing it.)*

STARBUCK. *(Evenly, gently)* Let 'em alone. They're all buttoned up fine. *(Circles to Left of her.)* As tight as they'll ever get— And it's a nice dress too. Brand new, ain't it? You expectin' somebody?

LIZZIE. None of your business.

STARBUCK. A woman gets all decked out—she must be expectin' her beau. Where is he? —it's gettin' kinda late.

LIZZIE. *(Breaking out)* I'm not expecting anybody! *(To Center.)*

STARBUCK. *(Quietly)* Oh I see. You were—but now you ain't. Stand you up?

LIZZIE. Mr. Starbuck, you've got more gall—! *(And she starts for the stairs. But he grabs her arm.)*

STARBUCK. Wait a minute!

LIZZIE. Let go of me!

STARBUCK. *(Tensely)* The question I really wanted to ask you before—it didn't have nothin' to do with buttons! It's this: The minute I walked into your house— you didn't like me! Why?!

LIZZIE. I said let go!

STARBUCK. *(Letting her go)* You didn't like me—why? Why'd you go up on your hind legs like a frightened mare?!

LIZZIE. I wasn't frightened, Mr. Starbuck! You paraded yourself in here—and you took over everything! I don't like to be taken by a con man!

STARBUCK. *(Lashing out)* Wait a minute! I'm sick and tired of this! I'm tired of you queerin' my work, callin' me out of my name!

LIZZIE. I called you what you are—a big-mouthed liar and a fake!

STARBUCK. *(With mounting intensity)* How do you know I'm a liar? How do you know I'm a fake? Maybe I *can* bring rain! Maybe when I was born God whis-

pered a special word in my ear! Maybe He said: "Bill
Starbuck, you ain't gonna have much in this world! You
ain't gonna have no wife and no kids—no green little
house to come home to! But Bill Starbuck—wherever
you go—you'll bring rain!" Maybe that's my one and
only blessing!

LIZZIE. *(To Left of sofa.)* There's no such blessing in
the world!

STARBUCK. *(Center.)* I seen even *better* blessings,
Lizzie-girl! I got a brother who's a doctor. You don't
have to tell him where you ache or where you pain! He
just comes in and lays his hand on your heart and pretty
soon you're breathin' sweet again! And I got another
brother who can sing—and when he's singin', that song
is *there!*—and never leaves you! *(With an outcry)* I
used to think—why ain't *I* blessed like Fred or Arny?
Why am I just a nothin' man, with nothin' special to my
name? And then one summer comes the drought—and
Fred can't *heal* it away and Arny can't *sing* it away! But
me—I go down to the hollow and I look up and I say:
"Rain! Dammit!—*please!*—bring rain!" And the rain
came! And I knew—I knew I was one of the family!

(She sits, Left end of sofa.)
(Suddenly quiet, angry with himself.) That's a story.
You don't have to believe it if you don't want to. *(He
sits, Right end of sofa.)*

LIZZIE. *(A moment. She is affected by the story—but
she won't let herself be. She pulls herself together with
some effort.)* I *don't* believe it!

STARBUCK. You're like Noah! You don't believe in
anything!

LIZZIE. That's not true!

STARBUCK. Yes it is! You're scared to believe in anything! You put the fancy dress on—and the beau don't
come! So you're scared that *nothin'll ever come!* You got
no faith!

LIZZIE. *(Crying out)* I've got as much as anyone!

STARBUCK. You don't even know what faith is! And
I'm gonna tell you! It's believin' you see white when

your eyes tell you black! It's knowin'—with your heart!

LIZZIE. And I know you're a fake.

STARBUCK. *(In sudden commiseration)* Lizzie, I'm sad about you. You don't believe in nothin'—not even in yourself! You don't even believe you're a woman. And if you *don't*—you're *not!* *(He turns on his heel and goes outdoors.)*

(LIZZIE *stands there, still hearing his words. She is deeply perturbed by them. The heat seems unbearable. From outdoors, the sound of the DRUM— boom—boom—boom.)*

LIZZIE. *(Upset—weakly)* Jimmy—please! Please— quit that!

(But he doesn't hear her. The DRUM continues. She rushes upstairs as the LIGHTS fade.)

(The LIGHTS come up inside FILE'S *office. The room is dimly illuminated by the gooseneck lamp on* FILE'S *desk and by the brilliant moonlight streaming through the window.* FILE *is lying on his leather couch staring unseeingly up at the ceiling. At last he gets up and stretches. He is unhappy and uncomfortable. He takes up a cardboard, fans himself once or twice and throws down the cardboard. The* SHERIFF *comes in.)*

FILE. Anything doin'?

SHERIFF. Not a thing—so I ran home for a while— Any calls?

FILE. *(Looking at a paper on his desk)* Peak's Junction called and said that Tornado Johnson fella was seen ridin' our way. Old lady Keeley called and said she heard thunder.

SHERIFF. How can she? She's deaf as a post.

FILE. I thought I heard it too. But it was too regular.

(Far in the distance, the sound of JIM's *DRUM.)*

SHERIFF. There it is!—Sure ain't thunder.

FILE. Lots of electricity in the air. My hair's full of it.

SHERIFF. Mine too. *(Watching him closely)* Phil Mackie says the Curry boys came by.

FILE. Oh yes— I forgot.

SHERIFF. Anything important?

FILE. —No.

SHERIFF. Phil says he saw Jim Curry come out of here wearin' a black eye.

FILE. He did, huh?

SHERIFF. Yeah—and he wasn't wearin' it when he came in— What happened?

FILE. *(With a flare of temper)* Tell Phil Mackie to mind his own damn business!

SHERIFF. *(Surprised—after a hurt instant)* And me to mind mine?

FILE. I'm sorry, Sheriff. *(A moody moment, then:)* Sheriff— I been thinkin'— I changed my mind.

SHERIFF. About what?

FILE. That dog you were talkin' about.

SHERIFF. You did, huh?

FILE. Yes. If the offer still holds, I'd sure like to have him.

SHERIFF. *(Embarrassed)* Well, I'll tell you, File— you said you didn't want him. And little Bobby Easterfield come over—and my wife gave him away— I'm sorry, File.

FILE. Forget it.

SHERIFF. What made you change your mind about the dog, File?

FILE. *(Evasively)* Oh, I don't know—

SHERIFF. Didn't have anything to do with the Currys, did it?

FILE. Now what the hell would my wantin' a dog have to do with the Currys, for God's sake?

SHERIFF. Well—didn't it?

FILE. *(After an instant.)* All right—it did!

SHERIFF. File, why don't you stop teasin' yourself? If you want to get yourself out of this stew—why don't you do it? Why don't you go over and see the Curry girl?

FILE. No! I ain't gonna be a dunce with a woman— not any more!

SHERIFF. Because you were a dunce with one of them —do you have to be a dunce with all of them?

FILE. I don't want to go over and see her—and just stand there like a stick!

SHERIFF. Don't stand! Sit down! Talk!

FILE. I make up conversations—and they all stay in my head!

SHERIFF. Well—flush 'em out!!

FILE. *(Suddenly making up his mind)* Mind if I take an hour off?

SHERIFF. Take two hours—take the whole night!

FILE. No—an hour's all I can stand!

(FILE *goes out. The* SHERIFF'S *eyes follow him with a pleased glance. The LIGHTS fade.)*

(The LIGHTS come up inside the living room which is momentarily unoccupied. From outdoors we hear the sound of JIM'S *DRUM. H.C. comes in through the door, carrying a whitewash brush and a pail of white paint. His face is daubed with whitewash as are his clothes. Bent nearly double from having been painting the arrow, he absent-mindedly sets the paint pail and brush down on the floor. Abruptly he realizes that the paint bucket will leave a mark and he snatches up the bucket and sets it outdoors. Re-entering quickly he looks at the floor now marked with paint. He scurries guiltily into the kitchen, grabs a towel and rushes back to clean up the mess. About to apply the spotless towel to the floor he realizes one doesn't get paint on a clean towel. He tosses the towel away, pulls out his shirt tail and kneels, applying the shirt tail to the floor.* NOAH *enters, unheard.* NOAH *has had discourteous treat-*

*ment by the recalcitrant mule; he is limping. He
stops at the sight of his father and watches H.C.
Then:)*

Noah. *(In doorway.)* He said paint the ground, not
the floor.

H.C. *(Right Center. Startled.)* I ain't paintin' the
floor—I'm cleanin' it.

(He rises and Noah gets a good look at him.)

Noah. Your face is all over whitewash.

H.C. Yep—I reckon it is.

Noah. So's your shirt.

H.C. Yep.

Noah. To look at you, you'd think you never painted
nothin' in your life.

H.C. *(Sheepishly)* I didn't see the bush.

Noah. What bush?

H.C. *(Annoyed.)* I was paintin' backward and suddenly there was that damn bush—and I bumped—and
the paint slopped all over everything!

*(Noah crosses the room, away from his father. H.C.
notices that Noah is limping.)*

H.C. What you limpin' about?

Noah. *(At cupboard up Left.)* I'm not limpin'!

H.C. Mule kick you? *(As Noah grunts, H.C. puts
brush on porch.)* Bad?

Noah. *(Annoyed)* Bad or good, a mule's kick is a
mule's kick. *(Sits at the table, working at his ledger.)*

*(Suddenly, from outdoors, louder than ever: BOOM
—BOOM—BOOM!)*

(Noah goes to the window and calls cholerically.) Jimmy, for Pete sake—come in here and quit beatin' that
drum!

(The DRUM stops.)

H.C. *(Smiles.)* I think he enjoys it.

NOAH. Sure. He's got the easiest job of all of us.

H.C. *(To Left of table; sits.)* Well, he's the lieutenant.

(JIM *enters, carrying the biggest bass drum in the world. He just stands there in the doorway, grinning. They stare at him. He beats the drum once, with a flourish, just for the hell of it.)*

NOAH. Jimmy, you quit that!

JIM. *(Puts drum by chest.)* He said for me to beat it every time I get the feelin'.

H.C. *(Tolerantly)* Well, Jimmy, if you can try to resist the feelin' we'll all appreciate it.

JIM. Holy mackerel, Pop, your face is all over whitewash.

H.C. *(Feigning surprise)* It is, is it?

JIM. Yeah—so's your shirt.

H.C. Well, whattaya know?

JIM. Whyn't you wash up? You look foolish.

H.C. You don't look so bright yourself, totin' that drum.

JIM. What am I gonna do with it?

NOAH. *(Exasperated.)* For the love of Mike, don't be so dumb!

JIM. *(Hurt and angry.)* Don't call me that, Noah!

(Silence. NOAH gets checkers from cupboard.)

H.C. I didn't notice—anybody see a cloud?

NOAH. Not a wisp of a one! And don't you expect it!

JIM. I wouldn't be so sure about that, Noah.

NOAH. You wouldn't—I would!

JIM. I think he *is* gonna bring rain! Because I been lookin' in his wagon. Boy, he's got all kinds of wheels and flags and a bugle and firecrackers—

NOAH. And all kinds of stuff that a con man would have—but nothin' that got anything to do with rain!

JIM. *(Crosses to chest.)* You're wrong, Noah. *(Opens the chest and take out a quilt and bed linen.)*

H.C. What are you doin' in Lizzie's linen chest?

JIM. *(Puts bedding on top of chest.)* He asked me could he spend the night in the tack room and I said yes. So I figured I'd get him somethin' to sleep on.

NOAH. You're sure stretchin' yourself to make him cozy, ain't you?

JIM. *(Above H.C., Left, eating grapes from table.)* Why not? I like him!

H.C. Funny—me too.

NOAH. *(Disgustedly)* He's certainly pullin' the wool over *your* eyes!

JIM. I'm out there with the drum—waitin' for the feelin' to come—and he comes over and we had a great talk, the two of us!

NOAH. What'd he try to sell you *this* time?

JIM. *(Leaning on H.C. In fervent defense of STAR-BUCK)* Nothin'!—he didn't try to sell me nothin'! He just come over—and I'm lookin' up at the sky—and he says: "What are you thinkin' about, Jim?" Real serious—like he gives a damn!

H.C. And what'd you tell him?

JIM. *(Importantly)* I said: "Not much."

H.C. Well, that's a good start to a conversation.

JIM. *(Crossing down Left)* And then before I know it, I'm tellin' him everything about myself! And I'm tellin' him about Lizzie and about how Noah snores at night! And I even told him about Snookie!

NOAH. Yeah?

JIM. Yeah! I says to him: "What do you think of a girl that wears loud clothes and puts lip rouge on her mouth and always goes around in a little red hat? Is she fast?" And you know what he said? *(On step Left; triumphantly)* He said: "Never judge a heifer by the flick of her tail!"

H.C. *(Suppressing a smile)* Sounds like sensible advice.

JIM. I think so! And then he says: "What do you think of the world?" And I say to him: "It's gonna get all *swole* up and bust right in our faces!" And you know what he told me? *(This, to him, is the most wonderful part.)* He said: "It's happened before—and it can happen again!" *(Crosses Right Center.)*

NOAH. There! I told you he'd sell you a bill of goods!

JIM. *(At door Right, angrily)* Noah, I understand that crack! You mean he was tryin' to make me feel smart -- and I ain't!

NOAH. Oh shut up!

JIM. No I won't shut up!

NOAH. What the hell's got into you?!

JIM. *(Above table Center, sits.)* I just thought of somethin', Noah. You know the only time I feel real dumb?

NOAH. When?

JIM. When I'm talkin' to you! Now why the hell *is* that, Noah?

(LIZZIE *comes down the stairs.*)

H.C. Lizzie—I thought you went to bed.

LIZZIE. It's roasting up there.

H.C. It's too bad we don't have one of those electric fans.

LIZZIE. It's not only the heat. Jimmy and his drum. *(Crosses up Right.)*

(The TELEPHONE rings. NOAH *answers it.* STARBUCK *appears at the Center window.)*

NOAH. Hello— Who?—No—he's not here. *(And summarily, he hangs up.)*

JIM. Who was that?

NOAH. Who else would have all that gall?

JIM. *(Rises.)* Snookie! Noah, that call was for me!

NOAH. Well?

JIM. *(Angry.)* Why'd you hang up on her?!

NOAH. Save you the trouble!

JIM. *(To Right of phone table.)* If she calls me on the

phone, you don't have to tell her I ain't here! I can do it myself!

NOAH. *(Left of him.)* How can you yourself tell her you ain't here?! Talk sense!

JIM. Maybe it don't make sense but you damn well know what I mean!

NOAH. *(Incensed)* Listen, Jimmy! If you want to get yourself in hot water—all you have to do is lift that phone and call her right back!

STARBUCK. *(Outside Center window, with studied casualness)* He's right, Jimmy. That's all you have to do.

NOAH. Stay out of this!

STARBUCK. I'm just agreeing with you, Noah. *(To JIM.)* You can call her right back.

> *(A moment of painful indecision on* JIM's *part. He looks at* STARBUCK *and at* NOAH, *who is standing squarely in front of the telephone.)*

(With quiet, urgent encouragement) Go on, kid.

JIM. *(Looking at* NOAH; *weakening)* I—I don't have her telephone number.

STARBUCK. All you have to do is call the operator.

JIM. *(Miserably—more plea than anger)* Let me alone, Starbuck!

STARBUCK. Go on!

> *(*JIM *turns away.)*

*(*STARBUCK *wheels around to* H.C.) H.C., a word from you might be a lot of help!

(JIM *is on step Left.)*

H.C. *(Quietly)* He'll work it out, Starbuck.

STARBUCK. *(Seeing that* H.C. *won't interfere, he moves quickly to* LIZZIE *at door Right.)* Lizzie! Tell Jimmy to make the call!

LIZZIE. *(With difficulty)* Starbuck, we'll all thank you not to interfere in our family.

STARBUCK. *(Squelched.)* Sorry— Guess I'm a damn

fool! *(Quickly, he turns on his heel and goes toward the tack room.)*

(There is a heavy silence in the room. NOAH crosses to Right. LIZZIE notices the quilt on chest.)

LIZZIE. What are these things doing here?

H.C. *(Indicating STARBUCK)* For Starbuck. Jimmy was going to take them out to the tack room—if it's all right.

LIZZIE. *(Takes quilt to JIM, Left.)* It's all right. Go on, Jimmy.

JIM. I don't want to now! *(And deeply upset, ashamed to face STARBUCK, ashamed to stay with the OTHERS, he hurries upstairs.)*

LIZZIE. *(Quietly)* You shouldn't have done that, Noah. *(Leaves quilt on newell post, then goes back to sofa.)*

NOAH. *(Guiltily—unhappily)* Somebody's gotta do it! *(Sits on chest.)*

LIZZIE. I think you liked doing it!

NOAH. No I didn't! *(In a hurt outburst)* For Pete sake—somebody take this family off my hands! I don't want to run it!

H.C. *(To up Right Center.)* You don't have to run the family, Noah—only the ranch.

NOAH. They're both tied up together! And if you don't like the way I do things—

H.C. *(Interrupting)* That ain't so, Noah! There's some things you do real good!

NOAH. *(In a pained outburst)* Then why don't you give me a little credit once in a while?! I'm tryin' to keep this family goin'! I'm tryin' to keep it from breakin' its heart on one foolishness after another! And what do I get for it!? Nothin' but black looks and complaints! *(Passionately)* Why—why?!

H.C. *(To Left of table.)* Because you're tryin' to run the family the way you run the ranch!

NOAH. There's no other way!

H.C. Noah, when I was your age I had my nose pressed

to the grindstone—just like you. Your mother used to say: "Let up, Harry—stop and catch your breath." Well, after she died I took her advice—on account of you three kids. And I turned around to enjoy my family. *(Quietly, urgently)* And I found out a good thing, Noah. If you let 'em live—people pay off better than cattle.

NOAH. *(In low anger)* Don't be so proud of the way you let us live, Pop. *(Pointing to LIZZIE)* Just look at *her*—and don't be so damn proud of yourself!

H.C. *(To Right Center. Angry and apprehensive)* What do you mean by that, Noah?

NOAH. *(Rises.)* Never mind!—you think about it! *(In cold fury, NOAH goes out Right.)*

(Long silence. When H.C. speaks to LIZZIE he doesn't look at her. There is heavy worry in his voice.)

H.C. What does he mean, Lizzie?

LIZZIE. *(Evasively)* I don't know— Don't pay any attention to him, Pop. *(She is itchy, restless. Her mood is mercurial, changing quickly between her yearning to find something new to do with herself—and her need to hide this yearning—perhaps by laughing at herself, by laughing at the world, by laughing at nothing at all.)* I don't know whether I'm hungry or thirsty. You like something to eat?

H.C. No, thanks. Noah's hinting that I made some big mistake with you, Lizzie. Did I?

LIZZIE. *(With surface laughter, with bravura)* Of course not. I'm perfect!—everybody knows I'm perfect! A very nice girl—good housekeeper, bright mind, very honest! So damn honest it kills me! How about a sandwich?

H.C. *(Puzzled by her mood. More definitely than before)* No, thanks.

LIZZIE. *You gotta get a man like a man gets got!* That's what Noah said. *(Laughing)* Now isn't that stupid? Why, it's not even good English!

H.C. *(Soberly)* Don't think about that, Lizzie. *(Sits Right of table.)*

LIZZIE. *(Protesting too much)* Think about it?—why, I wouldn't give it a second thought! *(Abruptly)* Pop, do you know what that Starbuck man said to me?!

H.C. *(Quietly)* What, Lizzie?

LIZZIE. No—why repeat it? A man like that—if you go repeating what people like that have to say—! *(Abruptly)* Why doesn't it rain?! What we need is a flood— *(With sudden gaiety)* —a great big flood—end of the world—ta-ta—goo'bye! *(Abruptly serious)* Pop, can a woman take lessons in being a woman?

H.C. You don't have to take lessons! You are one!

LIZZIE. *(Here it is!—the outcry.) Starbuck says I'm not!!!!*

H.C. *(A split second of surprise on* H.C.'s *part.)* —If Starbuck don't see the woman in you, he's blind!

LIZZIE. Is File blind? *Are they all blind? (Then, with deepening pain)* Pop, I'm sick and tired of *me!* I want to get out of *me* for a while—be somebody else!

H.C. Go down to the Social Club and be Lily Ann Beasley—is that what you want to be?

LIZZIE. Lily Ann Beasely knows how to get along!

H.C. Then you better call her on the telephone—ask her to let you join up!

LIZZIE. *(Defiantly)* I will!—you see if I don't! And I'm going to buy myself a lot of new dresses—cut way down to here! And I'll get myself some bright lip rouge —and paint my mouth so it looks like I'm always whistling!

H.C. Fine!—go ahead!—look like a silly little jackass!

LIZZIE. It won't be *me* looking silly—it'll be somebody else! You've got to hide what you are! You can't be honest!

H.C. *(Angrily)* You wouldn't know how to be anything else!

LIZZIE. Oh wouldn't I?—wouldn't I?! You think it's hard?—it's easy! Watch me—it's easy—look at this! *(She crosses the room, swinging her hips voluptuously.*

When she speaks it is with a silly, giggling voice—imitating Lily Ann. She addresses her father as if he were Phil Mackie, the town oaf.) Why, Phil Mackie!—how goodie-good-lookin' you are! Such curly blond hair, such pearly white teeth! C'n I count your teeth? One—two—three —four—nah—nah, mustn't bite! And all those muscle-ie muscles! Ooh, just hard as stone, that's what they are, hard as stone! Oh dear, don't tickle—don't tickle—or little Lizzie's gonna roll right over and dee-I-die! *(She is giggling uproariously.)*

(As she continues this makeshow game, she carries herself into convulsions of laughter. And H.C., seeing that she has unintentionally satirized the very thing she proposes to emulate, has joined her laughter. While this has been going on, they haven't noticed that FILE has appeared in the open doorway—and has witnessed most of LIZZIE's improvisation.)

FILE. Good evening.

(The laughter in the room stops. LIZZIE, at Left, is stock still in mortification.)

H.C. *(Rises to Center.)* Hello, File. Come in.

FILE. Kinda late. I hope I'm not disturbin' you.

H.C. No—no! We were just—well, I don't know *what* we were doin'—but come on in!

FILE. *(Entering to Center. Quietly)* Hello, Lizzie.

LIZZIE. Hello, File.

FILE. No—uh—no let-up in the drought, is there?

LIZZIE. Just—none—at all.

FILE. *(Uncomfortably—to H.C.)* H.C., I got to thinkin' about the little fuss I had with Jimmy and— about his eye and—well—I wanted to apologize. I'm sorry.

H.C. *(To Left of table, with a hidden smile)* You said that this afternoon, File.

FILE. But I didn't say it to Jim.

H.C. That's true—you didn't. (*With a quick look at* LIZZIE) He's upstairs—I'll send him down.

(*And quickly* H.C. *starts up the stairs. But* LIZZIE, *seeing it is her father's plan to leave her alone with* FILE, *takes a quick step toward the stairs and, all innocence, calls up to* JIM.)

LIZZIE. Oh, Jim—Jimmy—can you come down for a minute?

H.C. (*With studied casualness*) That's all right, Lizzie. —I was goin' up anyway.

(*And giving her no choice, he disappears from sight upstairs.* LIZZIE *and* FILE *are both aware of* H.C.'s *maneuver. They are both painfully embarrassed, unable to meet one another's glance.*)

LIZZIE. (*Just to fill the silence*) How about a cup of coffee?

FILE. No, thank you.—I already had my supper.

LIZZIE. (*Embarrassed at the mention of "supper"*) Yes —yes of course.

FILE. (*Seeing her embarrassment*) I didn't mean to mention supper—sorry I said it.

LIZZIE. (*Up Left Center.*) How about some nice cold lemonade?

FILE. No, thank you.

LIZZIE. (*In agony—talking compulsively*) I make lemonade with limes. I guess if you make it with limes you can't really call it *lemon*-ade, can you?

FILE. (*Generously—to put her at ease*) You can if you want to. No law against it.

LIZZIE. But it's really *lime*-ade, isn't it?

FILE. Yep—that's what it is, all right!

LIZZIE. (*Taking his mannish tone*) That's what it is, all right!

(*An impasse—nothing more to talk about. At last* JIM

*appears. He comes down the steps quickly—and he
is all grins that* FILE *is visiting.)*

JIM. You call me, Lizzie?—Hey, File.

FILE. Hello, Jim—- My, that's a bad eye. I came around
to say I'm sorry.

JIM. *(Delighted to have* FILE *here, he is all forgive-
ness. Crosses to him Center. Expansively:)* Oh, don't
think nothin' of it, File! Bygones is bygones!

FILE. Glad to hear you talk that way.

JIM. Sure—sure.

(An awkward silence.)

(JIM'S *grin fills the whole room. He looks from one to
the other, not knowing what to say, not knowing how
to get out. Abruptly)* Well—well! File's here, huh?
(Silence.)

(On a burst of enthusiasm) Yessir—he certain'y is!

*(And, in sheer happy animal spirits, he gives one loud
whack at the drum—and races out Right. He leaves
a vacuum behind him.)*

FILE. Was that Jim's drum I been hearin'?

LIZZIE. —Yes.

FILE. *(With a dry smile)* Didn't know he was musical.

LIZZIE. *(Smiling at his tiny little joke)* Uh—wouldn't
you like to sit down—or something?

FILE. No, thank you— *(Looking in the direction of*
JIM *and* H.C.) I guess they both knew I was lyin'.

LIZZIE. Lying? About what?

FILE. I didn't come around to apologize to Jim.

LIZZIE. What did you come for, File?

FILE. To get something off my chest. *(His difficulties
increasing)* This afternoon—your father—he—uh—
(Diving in) Well, there's a wrong impression goin' on
in the town—that I'm a widower. Well, I'm not!

LIZZIE. *(Quietly—trying to ease things for him. To
sofa; sits.)* I know that, File.

FILE. I know you know it—but I gotta say it! *(Blurting it out)* I'm a divorced man!

LIZZIE. You don't have to talk about it if you don't—

FILE. *(To Left Center, interrupting roughly)* Yes I do! I came to tell the truth! I've been denyin' that I'm a divorced man—well, now I admit it! That's all I want to say— *(Angrily)* —and that squares me with everybody!

LIZZIE. *(Soberly)* Does it?

FILE. Yes it does! And from here on in—if I want to live alone—all by myself—it's nobody's business but my own!

(He has said what he thinks he came to say. And having said it, he turns on his heel and starts to beat a hasty retreat. But LIZZIE stops him.)

LIZZIE. *(Sharply)* Wait a minute! *(As he turns, she rises; to Center chair.)* You're dead wrong!

FILE. Wrong? How?

LIZZIE. *(Hotly)* It's everybody's business!

FILE. How do you figure that, Lizzie?

LIZZIE. Because you owe something to people!

FILE. I don't owe anything to anybody!

LIZZIE. Yes you do!

FILE. What?!

LIZZIE. *(Inarticulate—upset)* I don't know—friendship! If somebody holds out his hand toward you, you've got to reach!—and take it!

FILE. *(To up Right Center.)* What do you mean I've got to?!

LIZZIE. *(In an outburst)* Got to! There are too many people alone—! And if you're lucky enough for somebody to want you—for a friend—! *(With a cry)* It's an *obligation!*

(Stillness. He is deeply disturbed by what she has said; even more disturbed by her impassioned manner.)

FILE. This—this ain't something the two of us can settle by just talkin' for a minute.

LIZZIE. *(Tremulously)* No—it isn't.

FILE. *(A move toward her.)* It'll take some time.

LIZZIE. —Yes. *(Sits on sofa.)*

(A spell has been woven between them. Suddenly it is broken by NOAH's entrance. Coming in by way of the front door, he is surprised to see FILE.)

NOAH. Oh, you here, File?

FILE. Yeah, I guess I'm here.

NOAH. *(Looking for an excuse to leave)* Uh—just comin' in for my feed book.

(He gets one of his ledgers from cupboard and goes out the front door. It looks as though the charmed moment is lost between them.)

FILE. *(Going to the door)* Well—

LIZZIE. *(Afraid he will leave.)* What were we saying?

FILE. What were *you* sayin'?

LIZZIE. *(Snatching for a subject that will keep him here)* I—you were telling me about your divorce.

FILE. No—I wasn't— *(Then, studying her, he changes his mind.)* —but I will. *(As he moves a step back into the room)* She walked out on me.

LIZZIE. I'm sorry.

FILE. Yes—with a schoolteacher. He was from Louisville.

LIZZIE. *(Helping him get it said)* Kentucky? *(As he nods)* Was she—I guess she was beautiful—?

FILE. *(A step toward her.)* Yes, she was.

LIZZIE. *(Her hopes dashed)* That's what I was afr— *(Catching herself)* —that's what I thought.

FILE. Black hair.

LIZZIE. *(Drearily, with an abortive little movement to her un-black hair)* Yes—black hair's pretty, all right.

FILE. I always used to think: If a woman's got pitch black hair she's already half way to bein' a beauty.

LIZZIE. *(Agreeing—but without heart)* Oh yes—-at least half way!

FILE. *(At Center chair. Suddenly, intensely, like a dam bursting)* With a schoolteacher dammit!—ran off with a schoolteacher!

LIZZIE. —What was *he* like?

FILE. *(Moves chair Left and sits. With angry intensity)* He had weak hands and nearsighted eyes!—and he always looked like he was about ready to faint!—and she ran off with *him!* And there *I* was—!

LIZZIE. *(Gently)* Maybe the teacher needed her and you didn't.

FILE. Sure I needed her!

LIZZIE. Did you tell her so?

FILE. *(Raging)* No I didn't! Why should I?!

LIZZIE. *(Astounded)* Why *should* you? Why *didn't* you?

FILE. Look here! There's one thing I've learned! *Be independent!* If you don't *ask* for things—if you don't let on you *need* things—pretty soon you *don't* need 'em!

LIZZIE. *(Desperately)* There are some things you *always* need!

FILE. *(Doggedly)* I won't ask for anything!

LIZZIE. But if you *had* asked her, she might have stayed!

FILE. I know darn well she mighta stayed! The night she left she said to me: "File, tell me not to go! Tell me don't go!"

LIZZIE. *(In wild astonishment)* And you didn't?!

FILE. I tried—I couldn't!

LIZZIE. Oh, pride—!

FILE. Look, if a woman wants to go. let her go! If you have to hold her back—*it's no good!*

LIZZIE. File, if you had to do it over again—

FILE. *(Interrupting, intensely)* I still wouldn't ask her to stay!

LIZZIE. *(In a rage against him)* Just *two words!*—
"don't go!"—you wouldn't say them?

FILE. It's not the words! It's beggin'—and I won't
beg!

LIZZIE. You're a fool!

*(It's a slap in the face. A dreadful moment for an
overly proud, stubborn man. A dreadful moment
for LIZZIE. It is a time for drastic measures—or he
will go. Having failed with FILE on an honest,
serious level, she seizes upon flighty falsity as a
mode of behavior. Precipitously, she becomes Lily
Ann Beasley, the flibbertigibbet. He rises; to up
Left Center.)*

(Chattering. With false, desperate laughter) Whatever
am I doing?—getting so serious with you, File! I shoulda
known better—because whenever I do, I put my foot
in it! Because bein' serious—that's not my nature! I'm
really a happy-go-lucky girl—just like any other girl
and I—would you like some grapes? *(Right of him,
hands him bowl from table.)*

FILE. *(Quietly)* No, thank you.

LIZZIE. *(Giddily)* They're very good! And so purply
and pretty! We had some right after supper! Oh, I wish
you'd been here to supper! I made such a nice supper!
I'm a good cook—and I just love cookin'! I think there's
only one thing I like better than cookin'! Readin' a
book! *(Gets book from sofa.)* Do you read very much?

FILE. *(Watching her as if she were a strange speci-
men)* No. Only legal circulars—from Washington.

LIZZIE. *(Left of him. Seizing on any straw to engage
him in the nonsensical chit-chat)* Oh, Washington!—I
just got through readin' a book about him! What a
great man! Don't you think Washington was a great
man?!

FILE. *(Drily)* Father of our country. *(Puts bowl back
on table.)*

LIZZIE. Yes—exactly! *(More Lily Ann Beasley than
ever)* Oh my!—what a nice tie! I just die for men in
black silk bow ties!

FILE. *(Quietly—getting angry)* It ain't silk—it's celluloid!

LIZZIE. No!—I can't believe it! It looks so real—it looks so real!

FILE. *(Significantly—like a blow)* It ain't real—it's fake!

LIZZIE. *(Unable to stop herself.)* And when you smile —you've got the strongest white teeth!

FILE. *(Angrily)* Quit that!

LIZZIE. *(Stunned)* What—?

FILE. *(Raging)* Quit it! Stop sashayin' around like a dumb little flirt!

LIZZIE. *(With a moan)* Oh no—

FILE. Silk tie—strong white teeth! What do you take me for? And what do you take yourself for?!

LIZZIE. *(In flight, in despair)* I was trying to—trying to—

FILE. Don't be so damn ridiculous! Be yourself!

(Saying which he leaves quickly Right. Alone, LIZZIE is at her wits' end—humiliated, ready to take flight from everything, mostly from herself. H.C. enters.)

H.C. *(Enters from upstairs.)* What happened, Lizzie?

JIM. *(Rushes in Right.)* What'd he do?—run out on you?! What happened?!

NOAH. *(Comes hurrying in from Right.)* I never seen a man run so fast! Where'd he go?

LIZZIE. *(Berserk—to all of them)* My God, were you watching a show? Did you think it was lantern slides?

JIM. What'd he say?

NOAH. What'd *you* say?

LIZZIE. I didn't say anything! Not one sensible thing! I couldn't even talk to him!

H.C. But you were talkin'!

LIZZIE. *(On floor, Right end of sofa.)* No! I was sashaying around like Lily Ann Beasley! I was making a fool of myself! Why can't I ever *talk* to anybody! ?

H.C. Lizzie, don't blame yourself! It wasn't your fault!

NOAH. *(Savagely)* No! It wasn't her fault—and it wasn't File's fault! *(Squaring off at his father)* And you know damn well whose fault it was!

H.C. *(On step Left.)* You mean it was mine, Noah?

NOAH. You bet it was yours!

LIZZIE. *(Seeing a fight—trying to head it off)* Noah—Pop—

H.C. No! He's got to explain that!

(At this point, STARBUCK appears at the Right doorway. He leans against the doorframe, silent, listening.)

NOAH. *(Accepting H.C.'s challenge)* I'll explain it all right! You been building up a rosy dream for her—and she's got no right to hope for it!

H.C. She's got a right to hope for anything!

NOAH. No! She's gotta face the facts—and you gotta help her face them! Stop tellin' her lies!

H.C. *(Crosses up Right.)* I never told her a lie in my life!

NOAH. You told her nothin' *but* lies! She's the smartest girl in the world! She's beautiful! And that's the worst lie of all! Because you know she's not beautiful! *She's plain!!*

JIM. Noah, you quit that!

NOAH. *(Whirling on JIM, up Left)* And you go right along with him! *(Whipping around to LIZZIE)* But you better listen to me! I'm the only one around here that loves you enough to tell you the truth! You're plain!

JIM. *(Violently)* Dammit, Noah—you quit it!

NOAH. *(To LIZZIE)* Go look at yourself in the mirror—you're plain!

JIM. Noah!

(Saying which, JIM hurls himself at his brother. NOAH falls into chair Left of Center table. But the instant he gets to him, NOAH strikes out with a tough fist. It

catches JIM *hard and he goes reeling. He returns with murder in his eye, but* NOAH *slaps him across the face, grabs the boy and forces him back to the table. Meanwhile, a frenetic outburst from* H.C. *and* LIZZIE:)

H.C. *and* LIZZIE. Noah—Jim—stop it! Stop it, both of you—stop it!

(And simultaneously, STARBUCK *rushes forward and breaks the two men apart. Out of* NOAH'S *grip,* JIM *goes berserk, bent on killing* NOAH. *But* STARBUCK *holds him off.)*

JIM. *(Through tears and rage)* Let me go, Starbuck—let me go!

STARBUCK. *(Holding* JIM *down Center)* Quit it, you damn fool—quit it!

JIM. *(With a cry)* Let go!

STARBUCK. Get outside! *(Letting him go)* Now go on—get outside!

JIM. *(Weeping)* Sure—I'll get outside! I'll get outside and never come back! *(And in on outburst of tears,* JIM *rushes out Right.)*

(LIZZIE *crosses to door Right.)*

NOAH. The next time that kid goes at me, I'll—I'll—

STARBUCK. The next time he goes at you, I'll see he has fightin' lessons!

NOAH. Look, you—clear out of here!

STARBUCK. No I won't clear out! And while I'm here, you're gonna quit callin' that kid a dumbbell!—because he's not! He can take a lousy little hickory stick—and he can see magic in it! But you wouldn't understand that!—because it's not in your books!

NOAH. *(To door Right)* I said clear out!

STARBUCK. *(Above* LIZZIE. *He cannot be stopped.)* And while I'm here, don't you ever call her plain!

Because you don't know what's plain and what's beautiful!

NOAH. Starbuck, this is family—it's not your fight!

STARBUCK. Yes it is! I been fightin' fellas like you all my life! And I always lose! But this time—by God, this time—!

(He reins himself in, then hurries out Right. We hear his voice calling "Jimmy!" NOAH breaks the stillness with quiet deliberateness:)

NOAH. *(To* LIZZIE *and* H.C.) I'm sorry I hit Jim—and I'll tell him so. But I ain't sorry for a single word I said to *her!*

H.C. *(Angry)* Noah, that's enough!

NOAH. *(Intensely)* No, it ain't enough! *(To* LIZZIE*)* Lizzie, you better think about what I said. Nobody's gonna come ridin' up here on a white horse. Nobody's gonna snatch you up in his arms and marry you. *You're gonna be an old maid!* And the sooner you face it, the sooner you'll stop breakin' your heart. *(He goes upstairs.)*

(Silence.)

LIZZIE. *(In doorway Right. Dully—half to herself)* Old maid—

H.C. Lizzie, forget it. Forget everything he said. *(To Left of table.)*

LIZZIE. No—he's right.

H.C. *(With a plea)* Lizzie—

LIZZIE. He's right, Pop. I've known it a long time. But it wasn't so bad until he put a name to it. Old maid. *(With a cry of despair)* Why is it so much worse when you put a name to it?

H.C. Lizzie, you gotta believe me—

LIZZIE. I don't believe you, Pop. You've been lying to to me—and I've been lying to myself!

H.C. Lizzie, honey—please—

LIZZIE. *(To chest.)* Don't—don't! I've got to see

things the way they are! And the way they will be! I've
got to start thinking of myself as a spinster! Jim will
get married! And one of these days, even Noah will get
married! I'll be the visiting aunt! I'll bring presents to
their children—to be sure I'm welcome! And Noah will
say: "Junior, be kind to your Aunt Lizzie—her nerves
aren't so good!" And Jim's wife will say: "She's been
visiting here a whole week now—when'll she ever go?!"
(With an outcry) Go where, for God's sake—go where?!

H.C. *(In pain for her)* Lizzie, you'll always have a
home. This house'll be *yours!*

LIZZIE. *(Crossing to stairs Left. Hysterically)* House
—house—house!

H.C. *(Right of her, trying to calm, to comfort her)*
Lizzie, stop it!

LIZZIE. Help me, Pop—tell me what to do!—help me!

H.C. Lizzie—Lizzie—!

*(To Right, then down front of stage, abruptly, without
thinking—in a frantic movement—she snatches up
the bed linens off the chest—and races outdoors.
The LIGHTS fade.)*

*(Brightest MOONLIGHT—moonlight alone—illumin-
ates the inside of the tack room. It is a rough, pic-
turesque room—a junk room really—at the rear of
the house. A slanting ceiling with huge hand-hewn
beams; a wagon wheel against a wall; leather goods
—saddles, horse traces and the like; a wagon seat
made into a bench. It is a room altogether acci-
dental, yet altogether romantic. STARUCK is pre-
paring to go to bed. He takes off his boots and his
neckerchief, then he stands in the Center of the
room, not moving, thinking intently. Gets feed
sacks, puts them on floor. It's stifling in here. He
takes his shirt off and sits on the edge of the seat,
suffering the heat. He waves his shirt around to
make a breeze. Opens the door at back. He lies down
on the sacks. The stillness is a palpable thing, and*

the heat. As he relaxes, as he slips back into his solitude, a lonely little humming comes from him. It grows in volume and occasionally we hear the words of the song. Suddenly he hears a sound and sits bolt upright.)

STARBUCK. Who's that? *(He rises tautly.)* Who's there?

LIZZIE. (LIZZIE *stands at rear of tack room, trying not to look into the room. She is carrying the bed linens. Trying to sound calm)* It's me—Lizzie.

(STARBUCK *starts to put on his shirt. An awkward moment. Then* LIZZIE, *without entering the room, hands him the bedding across the threshold.)*

Here.

STARBUCK. What's that?

LIZZIE. Bed stuff—take them.

STARBUCK. Is that what you came out for?

LIZZIE. *(After a painful moment)* No—I came out because— *(She finds it too difficult to continue.)*

STARBUCK. *(Gently)* Go on, Lizzie.

LIZZIE. I came out to thank you for what you said to Noah.

STARBUCK. I meant every word of it.

LIZZIE. What you said about Jim—I'm sure you meant that.

STARBUCK. What I said about you?

LIZZIE. I don't believe you.

STARBUCK. Lizzie! What are you scared of?

LIZZIE. You! I don't trust you!

STARBUCK. Why? What don't you trust about me?

LIZZIE. Everything! The way you talk, the way you brag—why, even your name!

STARBUCK. What's wrong with my name?

LIZZIE. It sounds fake! It sounds like you made it up!

STARBUCK. You're darn right! I did make it up!

LIZZIE. There! Of course!

STARBUCK. Why not? You know what name I was born with? Smith! Smith, for the love of Mike, *Smith!*

Now what kind of a handle is that for a fella like me! I needed a name that had the whole sky in it! And the power of a man! Star—buck! Now there's a name—and it's mine!

LIZZIE. No it's not! You were born Smith—and that's your name!

STARBUCK. You're wrong, Lizzie! The name you choose for yourself is more your own than the name you were born with! And if I was you I'd sure choose another name than Lizzie!

LIZZIE. Thank you—I'm very pleased with it!

STARBUCK. Oh no you ain't! You ain't pleased with anything but yourself! And I'm sure you ain't pleased with "Lizzie"!

LIZZIE. I don't ask *you* to be pleased with it, Star-buck. *I am!*

STARBUCK. Lizzie! Why, it don't *stand* for anything!

LIZZIE. It stands for me! *Me!* I'm not the Queen of Sheba—I'm not Lady Godiva—I'm not Cinderella at the Ball!

STARBUCK. Would you like to be?

LIZZIE. Starbuck, you're ridiculous!

STARBUCK. What's ridiculous about it? Dream you're somebody—be somebody! But Lizzie?—that's nobody! So many millions of wonderful women with wonderful names! *(In an orgy of delight)* Leonora, Desdemona, Caroline, Annabella, Florinda, Christina, Diane! *(Then with a pathetic little lift of his shoulders)* Lizzie.

LIZZIE. Goodnight, Starbuck!

STARBUCK. *(With a sudden inspiration)* Just a min-ute, Lizzie—just one little half of a minute! I got the greatest name for you—the greatest name—just listen! *(Then, like a love lyric)* Melisande.

LIZZIE. *(Flatly)* I don't like it.

STARBUCK. That's because you don't know anything about her! But when I tell you who she was—lady, when I tell you who she was!

LIZZIE. Who?

STARBUCK. She was the most beautiful—! She was

the beautiful wife of King Hamlet!—Ever hear of him?

LIZZIE. *(Giving him rope)* Go on!—go on!

STARBUCK. He was the fella who sailed across the ocean and brought back the Golden Fleece! And you know why he did that? Because Queen Melisande begged him for it! I tell you, that Melisande—she was so beautiful and her hair was so long and curly—every time he looked at her he just fell right down and died! And this King Hamlet, he'd do anything for her—anything she wanted! So when she said: "Hamlet, I got a terrible hankerin' for a soft Golden Fleece," he just naturally sailed right off to find it! And when he came back—all bleedin' and torn—he went and laid that Fleece of Gold right down at her pretty white feet! And she took that fur piece and she wrapped it around her pink naked shoulders and she said: "I got the Golden Fleece—and I'll never be cold no more!"—Melisande! What a woman! What a *name!!*

LIZZIE. *(Forlornly)* Starbuck, you silly jackass. You take a lot of stories—that I've read in a hundred different places—and you roll them up into one big fat ridiculous lie!

STARBUCK. *(Angry, hurt.)* I wasn't lyin'—I was dreamin'!

LIZZIE. It's the same thing!

STARBUCK. If you think it's the same thing then I take it back about your name! Lizzie—it's just right for you! I'll tell you another name that would suit you— Noah! Because you and your brother—you've got no dream!

LIZZIE. *(With an outcy)* You think all dreams have to be your kind! Golden fleece and thunder on the mountain! But there are other dreams, Starbuck! Little quiet ones that come to a woman when she's shining the silverware and putting moth flakes in the closet!

STARBUCK. Like what?

LIZZIE. Like a man's voice saying: "Lizzie, is my blue suit pressed?" And the same man saying: "Scratch between my shoulder blades." And kids laughing and teasing and setting up a racket! And how it feels to say the word "Husband"!—There are all kinds of dreams, Mr. Starbuck! Mine are small ones—like my name—Lizzie! But they're *real* like my name—real! So you can have yours—and I'll have mine! *(Unable to control her tears.)*

STARBUCK. *(This time he grabs her fully, holding her close.)* Lizzie—

LIZZIE. Please—

STARBUCK. I'm sorry, Lizzie! I'm sorry!

LIZZIE. It's all right—let me go!

STARBUCK. I hope your dreams come true, Lizzie—I hope they do!

LIZZIE. They won't—they never will!

STARBUCK. Believe in yourself and they will!

LIZZIE. I've got nothing to believe in!

STARBUCK. You're a woman! Believe in that!

LIZZIE. How can I when nobody else will?

STARBUCK. *You* gotta believe it first! *(Quickly)* Let me ask you, Lizzie—are you pretty?

LIZZIE. *(With a wail)* No—I'm plain!

STARBUCK. There! You see?—you don't know you're a woman!

LIZZIE. I am a woman! A plain one!

STARBUCK. There's no such thing as a plain woman! Every real woman is pretty! They're all pretty in a different way—but they're all pretty!

LIZZIE. Not me! When I look in the looking glass—

STARBUCK. Don't let Noah be your lookin' glass! It's gotta be inside you! And then one day the lookin' glass will be the man who loves you! It'll be his eyes maybe! And you'll look in that mirror and you'll be more than pretty!—you'll be beautiful!

LIZZIE. *(Crying out)* It'll never happen!

STARBUCK. Make it happen! Lizzie, why don't you think "pretty"? and take down your hair! *(He reaches for her hair.)*

LIZZIE. *(In panic)* No!

STARBUCK. Please, Lizzie! *(He is taking the pins out*

of her hair. Taking her in his arms) Now close your eyes, Lizzie—close them! *(As she obeys)* Now—say: I'm pretty!

LIZZIE. *(Trying)* I'm—I'm—I can't!

STARBUCK. Say it! Say it, Lizzie!

LIZZIE. I'm—pretty.

STARBUCK. Say it again!

LIZZIE. *(With a little cry)* Pretty!

STARBUCK. Say it—mean it!

LIZZIE. *(Exalted)* I'm pretty! I'm pretty! I'm pretty! *(He kisses her. A long kiss and she clings to him, passionately, the bonds of her spinsterhood breaking away. The kiss over, she collapses on the sacks, sobbing.)*

(Through the sobs) Why did you do that?!

STARBUCK. *(Going beside her on the sacks)* Because when you said you were pretty, it was true!

(Her sobs are louder, more heartrending because, for the first time, she is happy.)

Lizzie—look at me!

LIZZIE. I can't!

STARBUCK. *(Turning her to him)* Stop cryin' and look at me! Look at my eyes! What do you see?

LIZZIE. *(Gazing through her tears)* I can't *believe* what I see!

STARBUCK. Tell me what you see!

LIZZIE. *(With a sob of happiness)* Oh, is it me?! Is it really me?! *(Now she goes to him with all her giving.)*

END OF ACT TWO

ACT THREE

SCENE: *The LIGHTS come up inside the house to reveal*
H.C. at the telephone.

H.C. *(Into phone)* Thank you, Howard— I'm sorry
I woke you up— Well, if you hear from Jimmy, you
call me right away, will you? No, nothin's wrong—
Thank you.

(He hangs up and paces worriedly. NOAH comes down
the stairs wearing his bathrobe. He has been unable
to sleep a wink.)

NOAH. *(On stairs, grumpily)* Jimmy get home yet?
H.C. *(Up Center.)* Nope.
NOAH. That dopey kid. It's near two o'clock.
H.C. Go back to sleep, Noah. Don't worry about him.
NOAH. I ain't worryin' about him. I don't give a damn
what happens to him.
H.C. Okay—fine.
NOAH. Maybe he's at the Hopkinson's— I'll call them.
H.C. I called them all. Nobody seen him.
NOAH. If you'da seen my side of this, it wouldn't of
happened.
H.C. *(Then sits Right of table.)* I see your side,
Noah—I just ain't *on* your side.
NOAH. *(Angrily)* Nobody is! *(Exits upstairs.)*

(KLAXON off Left. NOAH re-enters. At this instant, JIM
stands in the doorway. He looks very cocky, very
self-satisfied, ten feet taller than before. He is
smoking an enormous cigar with an air of aloof
grandeur. He struts majestically.)

JIM. Good e-ve-ning!

NOAH. Where the hell you been?

JIM. *(In door Right. With a lordly gesture)* Out—out —out!

NOAH. What's wrong with you? Are you drunk?

JIM. *(With an air of superiority)* No, Big Brother, I ain't drunk. But if I cared to be drunk, I'd be google-eyed! *(Crosses to Left.)*

H.C. *(Secretly amused)* Where'd you get the stogie, Jim?

JIM. *(Left of H.C.)* It ain't a stogie. It's a Havana Panatella. Eighty-five cents. And it's a present.

NOAH. Who the hell gave it to you?

JIM. I-the-hell gave it to me!—For bein' a big boy!

NOAH. You didn't tell us where you been.

JIM. *(Circling around room)* I don't have to—but I will. I been out with my favorite girl— *(He takes a little red hat out of his pocket, unfolds it and slaps it on his head. Sits astride chair Right of table.)* —Snookie!

NOAH. You crazy, dumb little—

JIM. *(Warningly—with an even smile)* Uh-uh-uh-uh! Don't say dumb no more, Noah. Or I shall take this eighty-five cent Havana Panatella and I shall squash it right in your mean old face!

H.C. *(Sits on sofa.)* What happened, Jimmy?

NOAH. Can't you see what happened? He went ridin' with Snookie Maguire and she got him all hot up and then, by God, she trapped him!

JIM. Big Brother, you got it all wrong!

NOAH. Don't lie to me, Jimmy Curry! The minute I stopped lookin' after you, you got yourself in trouble! *(Rises to porch, then Left to sofa; sits in Center chair, then rises to above Left Center.)*

JIM. Noah, when I tell you what *really* happened, you're gonna split your britches! We went ridin'—yep, that's right! We opened that Essex up and we went forty million miles an hour! And then we stopped that car and we got out and we sat down under a great big tree! And we could look through the branches and see the sky all full of stars—*damn, it was* full of stars! And I turned around and I kissed her! I kissed her once, I kissed her a hundred times! And while I was doin' that, I knew I could carry her anywhere—right straight to the moon! But all the time, I kept thinkin': "Noah's gonna come along and he's gonna say 'Whoa!' " But Noah didn't show up—and I kept right on kissin'! And then somethin' happened! *She* was cryin' and *I* was cryin' and I thought any minute now we'll be right up there on the moon! And then—then!—without Noah bein' there— all by my smart little self—*I said Whoa!*

H.C. *(Circles Right of* Jim.*)* Yippeeeeee!

Jim. *(Formally)* Thank you, Pop—your yippee is accepted.

Noah. *(Center.)* I don't believe a word of it. Why'd she give you the hat?

Jim. For the same reason I give her my elk's tooth! We're engaged.

Noah. *(Up Right Center.)* So I was right. She did trap you!

Jim. *(Warningly, Left Center)* Noah, I see I'm gonna have to give you this Havana Panatella.

H.C. Don't listen to him, Jimmy. Congratulations.

(They shake hands.)

Jim. *(Touched.)* Thanks, Pop—thank you very kindly. *(Suddenly elated)* I gotta tell Lizzie! Where's Lizzie?!

Noah. Where the Sam Hill do you think she is? She's asleep!

Jim. *(Hurrying to the stairs)* Well, then, I'll wake her up!

H.C. *(Up to window Center.)* Wait, Jimmy— Lizzie's not up there.

Jim. Where is she?

(A moment.)

Noah. *(In door Right.)* Where is she, Pop?
H.C. She's out in the tack room.

Noah. You mean with Starbuck?

H.C. Yes.

Jim. *(On step Left.)* Boy that's great! *(Pulling another cigar out of his pocket)* I got another cigar for Lizzie!

Noah. *(To up Right Center. Quietly to H.C.)* Wait a minute. You mean you let her walk in on that fella when he's sleepin'? You didn't even try to stop her!

H.C. *(Left of table.)* No I didn't! You called her an old maid! You took away the last little bit of hope she ever had! And when you left, she lifted up those bed linens and ran out! I didn't ask her where she was goin' —but I'm glad she went! Because if she lost her hope in here—maybe she'll find it out there!

Noah. That was in your mind the minute you laid eyes on that fella!

H.C. You put it awful cut and dried, Noah.

Noah. It's the truth!

Jim. Well, what of it? I think it's great them bein' out there together! They might get real serious about each other! And before you know it, I got me a new brother! Boy, I'd swap him for you any day!

Noah. *(Crosses up Left Center.)* You won't have to swap him for anybody! Because he ain't the marryin' kind—not that faker!

Jim. *(Crosses Center to H.C.)* I bet he is the marryin' kind—I bet he is! Hey Pop, what do you figure a rainmaker makes?

H.C. *(Soberly)* Don't let's be beforehand, Jimmy. *(Then to up Right Center.)*

(Suddenly there, on the threshold, FILE and the SHERIFF. FILE knocks on the door frame.)

FILE. Mind if we come in, H.C.?

H.C. Hello, File— Hey, Sheriff—come on in.

Noah *and* Jim. Hey, File— Hey, Sheriff.

H.C. Kinda late to be visitin' ain't it, Sheriff?

Sheriff. Well, we're not exactly visitin', H.C.

FILE. *(Crossing down Center)* How's Lizzie?

H.C. Fine, boy, fine. *(With a trace of puzzled amusement)* You just seen her a little while ago.

FILE. *(With a little embarrassment)* Yeah––I know.

H.C. *(Crosses to sofa.)* You and the Sheriff come callin' on Lizzie?

FILE. *(Quickly)* No—uh—no.

H.C. *(Picking up newspaper)* What can I do for you?

FILE. *(On floor Left, crosses to above sofa.)* I'll tell you, H.C. We been gettin' a lot of phone calls from Pedleyville and Peak's Junction and all down the state line. They been lookin' for a fella––well, he's a kinda con man. Name of Tornado Johnson— *(But he can't get his mind off* LIZZIE.) She asleep?

H.C. *(Baiting him goodnaturedly)* Who—Lizzie?

FILE. Well, I reckon she is— You get any wind of him?

H.C. Who?

FILE. *(Irritably)* Tornado Johnson.

H.C. *(Sits on sofa.)* Nope.

FILE. *(Referring to a "Wanted" circular he has brought with him)* Tornado Johnson—alias Bill Harmony—alias Bill Smith.

H.C. I never met anybody called himself by any of those names.

FILE. *(Up Left Center.)* Anybody else come around here?

H.C. *(Smiling)* Only you, File.

FILE. *(Looking toward the stairs)* Kind of a hot night to be asleep, ain't it?

H.C. Lizzie's a good sleeper.

FILE. Yeah—must be.

SHERIFF. *(To Right of* H.C.) No Tornado Johnson, huh?

H.C. Nope.

SHERIFF. *(Sits Center chair.)* Seems a little fishy.

JIM. *(On chest Right Center.)* How do you mean fishy?

SHERIFF. Well, Pedleyville and the Junction and Three

Point—we all kinda figured this together and—uh—
(Embarrassed, he looks at FILE.*)*

FILE. Look, H.C., we know it ain't like you to protect a criminal.

NOAH. *(Up Right Center, quickly)* Really a criminal, huh?

FILE. *(Uncomfortably)* Well, he's wanted!

H.C. What's he wanted for, File?

(NOAH *and* JIM *cross to above sofa, Left of* FILE.)

FILE. *(Referring to the "Wanted" bulletin again)* He's wanted in the state of Kansas. He sold four hundred tickets to a great big Rain Festival. No rain, no festival!

SHERIFF. In a small town in Nebraska he drummed up a lot of excitement about what he called a Spectacular Eclipse of the Sun—and he peddled a thousand pair of smoked eyeglasses to see it with. No eclipse.

FILE. In the month of February he sold six hundred wooden poles. He called them Tornado Rods. Claimed that if that town ever got hit by a tornado the wind would just blow through there like a gentle spring breeze —and not hurt a thing. Well, when he left, the town got hit by every blow you can imagine—windstorm, hailstorm, cyclone and hurricane! Blew the Tornado Rods off the roof and blew the town off the map!

(NOAH *to Right of table Center.*)

JIM. *(Left of* FILE.*)* Did it ever get hit by a tornado?

FILE. No, it didn't.

JIM. Well, that's all he guaranteed—that it wouldn't get hit by a tornado! And it didn't!

H.C. Don't sound like a criminal to me, File.

SHERIFF. No, he don't—but we gotta do *somethin'* about him—we ain't locked anybody up for three weeks.

H.C. *(With a smile)* Sorry I can't help you, Sheriff.

FILE. I got a feelin' you can. They say this fella carries a great big bass drum wherever he goes. Whose drum is that?

JIM. It's mine. I'm figurin' to be a drummer.

FILE. Who painted that big white arrow on the ground?

H.C. I did!

FILE. What do *you* figure to be, H.C.—a whitewash painter?

H.C. Maybe.

FILE. *(Taking a step up toward the window)* Yeah? Whose wagon is that?

(Silence.)

SHERIFF. *(Rises; to door Right.)* Let's go have a look at that wagon, File.

(FILE *and the* SHERIFF *quickly go out Right.)*

NOAH. *(To Left Center. In an outburst, to* H.C.*)* Why'd you do that? Why the hell did you do that?

H.C. *(To Center. Upset.)* I don't know.

NOAH. Why didn't you tell them—straight out: "The fella you're lookin' for is in the tack room with my daughter!"?

H.C. *(To Right Center.)* Because he's with my daughter!

NOAH. *(With angry resolve)* All right! I didn't tell them you were lyin'!—I stood by you! But I ain't standin' by you any more! *(He starts for the door.)*

H.C. Where you goin', Noah?

NOAH. I'm goin' out to the tack room and bring her in!

H.C. Noah, wait!

NOAH. *(Crosses Left to cupboard.)* And I'm gonna bring him in too!

H.C. He's a quick fella, Noah—and you're a little slow on your feet!

NOAH. *(Opens cupboard drawer and brings out a gun.)* I'll be quicker with this!

H.C. *(Angry.)* Put that down!

NOAH. *(Left Center.)* You want Lizzie out there with him?! He's a swindler and a crook and I don't know what else!

H.C. I'll tell you what else, Noah—he's a man!

JIM. *(On step Right.)* Pop's right! Gettin' married is gettin' married!

H.C. Jimmy, you always say the smart thing at a dumb time!

JIM. Well, I'm all for her gettin' married—I don't care who the fella is!

NOAH. Is that the way you think, Pop?

H.C. You know it's not the way I think!

NOAH. Then I'm goin'!

H.C. I said stay here!

NOAH. *(Center, at table. Raging)* It ain't right, Pop— it ain't right!

H.C. *(Exploding)* Noah, you're so full of what's right you can't see what's *good!* It's good for a girl to get married, sure—but maybe you were right when you said she won't ever have that! Well, she's gotta have somethin'! *(With desperate resolution)* Lizzie has got to have somethin'! Even if it's only one minute—with a man talkin' quiet and his hand touchin' her face! And if you go out there and shorten the time they have together—if you put one little dark shadow over the brightest time of Lizzie's life—I swear I'll come out after you with a whip! *(Quietly)* Now you give me that gun!

(A taut moment during which NOAH and H.C. confront each other in open hostility. NOAH is too righteously proud to give the gun to his father, yet not strong enough to defy him. At last, to give in without entirely losing face, he puts the gun back in the drawer. The LIGHTS fade.)

(The LIGHTS come up inside the tack room. STARBUCK *and* LIZZIE *are sitting on the sacks, leaning against the back of the buggy seat. They are quite intimately close, looking out through the open door at the bright expanse of sky.* LIZZIE *has the shine of moonlight over her face and this glow, meeting her inner radiance, makes her almost beautiful.)*

STARBUCK. And I always walk so fast and ride so far I never have time to stop and ask myself no question.

LIZZIE. If you did stop, what question would you ask?

STARBUCK. Well—I guess I'd say: "Big Man, where you goin'?"

LIZZIE. *(Quietly)* Big Man, where *are* you going?

STARBUCK. *(After an indecisive moment)* I don't know— I reckon I better kiss you again. *(He kisses her and they are close for a moment.)* Didn't anybody ever kiss you before I did, Lizzie?

LIZZIE. *(With a wan smile)* Yes—once.

STARBUCK. When was that?

LIZZIE. I was about twelve, I guess. There was a boy with freckles and red hair—and I thought he was the beginning of the world! But he never paid me any mind. Then one day he was standing around with a lot of other boys. And suddenly, he shot over to me and kissed me hard, right on the mouth! And for a minute I was so stirred up—! But then he ran back to the other kids and I heard him say: "I'll kiss anything on a dare— even your old man's pig!"—So I ran home and up the back stairs and I locked my door and looked at myself in the mirror—and from that day on I knew I was plain.

STARBUCK. Are you plain, Lizzie?

LIZZIE. *(Looking at him, smiling)* No—I'm beautiful.

STARBUCK. You are—and when I leave here, don't you ever forget it!

LIZZIE. *(A little sadly; reconciled to his ultimate going)* I'll try to remember—everything—you ever said.

STARBUCK. *(Rises restively. Somehow he is deeply disturbed, lonely. He walks to the door, his back to* LIZZIE,

*and looks out at the night. There is searching in his face,
and yearning. At last it comes out in a little outcry:)*
Lizzie, I want—I want to live forever!

LIZZIE. *(Full of compassion.)* I hope you do—wherever you are—I hope you do!

STARBUCK. You don't say that as if you think I'll ever get what I'm after.

LIZZIE. *(Gently)* I don't really *know* what you're after.

STARBUCK. I'm after a clap of lightnin'! I want things to be as pretty when I *get* them as they are when I'm *thinkin'* about them!

LIZZIE. *(Hurt. He seems to disparage the moment of realization they've had together.)* I think they're prettier when you get them.

STARBUCK. No! Nothin's as pretty in your hands as it was in your head! There ain't no world near as good as the world I got up here!—Why??

LIZZIE. I don't know. Maybe it's because you don't take time to see it. Always on the go—here, there, nowhere. Runnin' away—keepin' your own company. Maybe if you'd keep company with the *world*—

STARBUCK. *(Doubtfully)* I'd learn to love it?

LIZZIE. You might—if you saw it *real!* Some nights I'm in the kitchen washing the dishes. And Pop's playing poker with the boys. Well, I'll watch him real close. And at first I'll just see an ordinary middle-aged man—not very interesting to look at. And then, minute by minute, I'll see little things I never saw in him before. Good things and bad things—queer little habits I never noticed he had. And suddenly I know who he is!—and I love him so much I could cry! And I want to thank God I took the time to see him *real!*

STARBUCK *(Breaking out)* Well, I ain't got the time!

LIZZIE. Then you ain't got no world—except the one you make up in your head.

STARBUCK. *(A long moment. When at last he speaks, it is with painful difficulty.)* Lizzie—I got somethin' to tell you— You were right— I'm a liar and a con man and a fake! *(A moment. The words tear out of him.)* I never made rain in my life!—Not a single raindrop!—nowhere!—not anywhere at all!

LIZZIE. *(In a compassionate whisper)* I know—

STARBUCK. All my life—wantin' to make a miracle!—Nothin'!—I'm a great big blowhard!

LIZZIE. *(Gently)* No— You're all dreams. And it's no good to live in your dreams!

STARBUCK. It's no good to live outside them either!

LIZZIE. Somewhere between the two—

STARBUCK. Yes!—Lizzie, would you like me to stick around for a while?

LIZZIE. *(Unable to stand the joy of it.)* Did I hear you right?

STARBUCK. Not for good, understand—just for a few days!

LIZZIE. You're—you're not fooling me, are you, Starbuck?

STARBUCK. No—I mean it!

LIZZIE. *(Crying)* Would you stay? Would you?

STARBUCK. A few days—yes!

LIZZIE. *(Her happiness bursting)* Oh! Oh my goodness! Oh!

STARBUCK. Lizzie—

LIZZIE. I can't stand it—I just can't stand it!

STARBUCK. *(Taking her in his arms)* Lizzie—

LIZZIE. You look up at the sky and you cry for a star! You know you'll never get it! And then one night you look down—and there it is—shining in your hand! *(Half laughing, half crying, she goes into his arms again as the LIGHTS fade. She crosses downstage to Right, then enters house Right door.)*

(The LIGHTS come up inside the house where H.C. and NOAH are waiting for things to come to pass. NOAH is at Left of table working at his books. H.C. is seated on chest. A restless tension in the room.)

(LIZZIE enters through the Right door. The moonlight

still glows on her. NOAH *and* H.C. *turn, their eyes fixed on the girl.* LIZZIE *looks from one to another, trying to contain the rhapsody in her.)*

NOAH. *(To up Left Center.)* Where's Starbuck?

LIZZIE. In the tack room. *(Unable to speak in front of* NOAH, *she shifts nervously to:)* You know—I think I saw a wisp of a cloud— *(Her happiness bursting forth)* —no bigger than a mare's tail!

NOAH. She's talkin' like him!

LIZZIE. *(Sits Center chair.)* Yes—I am—yes!

NOAH. Whyn't you comb your hair?

LIZZIE. *(With an excited laugh)* I like it this way! I'm going to wear it this way all my life! I'm going to throw away my pins! *(Taking a handful of pins out of her pocket she tosses them high in the air.)* There! I've got no more pins! *(Then, in a rush to her father)* But I've got something else!

H.C. *(Quietly)* What, Lizzie?

LIZZIE. Pop— Oh Pop, I've got me a beau!

H.C. *(Heavily, trying to smile)* Have you, honey?

LIZZIE. Not an always beau—but a beau for meanwhile! Until he goes! He says he'll go in a few days— but anything can happen in a few days—anything can happen! *(Ecstatically; to Left, then to doorway Right.)* Oh Pop, the world's turned clear around!

NOAH. Why don't you tell her, Pop?

LIZZIE. Tell me what?

H.C. *(With difficulty)* Lizzie, you were right about that fella. He's a liar and a con man.

LIZZIE. *(With a cry)* But there's nothing bad about him, Pop! He's so good—and so alone—he's so terribly alone! *(On floor by* H.C.)

NOAH *(Going to the Center window—not unkindly)* Lizzie—come here.

LIZZIE. What?

NOAH. Look out this window.

LIZZIE *(She crosses to the window and looks out. A moment of bewilderment and dread.)* What are they here for? What are they doing on his wagon? *(As* NOAH *turns away)* Pop!

H.C. *(To Center.)* They're gettin' evidence against him, Lizzie. The Sheriff's here to lock him up.

LIZZIE. No!

(Suddenly she starts for the door but NOAH *stops her.)*

NOAH. Stay here, Lizzie!

LIZZIE. Let me go, Noah! *(In a panic, to* H.C.*)* They've got no right to arrest him!

H.C. Yes they have.

LIZZIE. Pop, we've got to help him!

H.C. *(Painfully)* Lizzie, quit it! There's nothin' we can do for him!

LIZZIE. *(Moves up Right.)* Not for him—for me!

H.C. *(Left of her.)* For you, Lizzie? I don't think he knows who you are! I think he dreamed you up in his head!

LIZZIE. No! He sees me as real as you do!

H.C. Do you believe that, Lizzie? Do you think he sees you real? *(As she hesitates)* Answer me!

LIZZIE. *(A painful moment—then—)* Yes, he does!

H.C. All right then—you better help him get away! Go out the back door and—

(She starts Left.)

NOAH. You're not gonna let her do that, Pop! *(He crosses to kitchen.)*

H.C. Yes! I am!

NOAH. No! I won't let you!

*(*NOAH *stands there, barring the door.* LIZZIE, *in a wild flight, starts for the Right door. But just as she reaches it,* FILE *and* JIM *enter, blocking the doorway. A taut moment.)*

FILE. Well—you awake?

LIZZIE. Hello, File.

FILE. They said you were asleep.

LIZZIE. Did they? *(Trying to get past him)* Excuse me.

FILE. *(Blocking her path)* Where you goin', Lizzie?

LIZZIE. *(Afraid of giving STARBUCK away.)* Nowhere. Outside.

FILE. *(Suspiciously)* Wait a minute, Lizzie! What are you in such a rush for?

LIZZIE. *(Confused.)* I—I just wanted to see what you were doing out there—on that wagon!

FILE. *(To Center)* Well, I came in now. So you don't have to go out. *(Shrewdly—quickly)* Unless there's *some* other reason for you goin'?

LIZZIE. No—no.

FILE. *(To the OTHERS—his eye on LIZZIE)* I guess we got what we came for. All right, H.C.—where is he? *(To up Right.)*

H.C. *(Left Center at table.)* Do your own work, File.

FILE. *(Circles above Center.)* H.C. I don't want this family mixed up in trouble. Tell me where he is—please!

JIM. He left about an hour ago!

FILE. Where'd he go?

JIM. *(On chest Right Center.)* Pedleyville!

FILE. *(Center.)* How'd he go? His wagon's still here!

H.C. He took Jim's roan!

JIM. Yeah—he took my roan!

FILE. I think you're lyin'—all of you! *(With sudden enraged exasperation)* What the hell's goin' on here anyway? I ask you questions and you tell me a pack of lies! *(Circles around sofa; crosses to LIZZIE.)* And for what?! A stranger!—a man who don't mean anything to you! *(Abruptly he goes still as the thought assails him:)* Or does he?! *(As he feels the tautness of the silence, his attention slowly, slowly turns to LIZZIE. Slowly, slowly he crosses the room and places himself squarely facing her.)* Maybe *you* better answer that question, Lizzie.

(It is too much for her. She takes a quick step away

to Right Center, in flight—but FILE *grabs her.)*
(Center.) No—wait a minute! They said you were
asleep—but you weren't! Why did they lie about that?
Where were you, Lizzie?

LIZZIE. *(Painfully)* It has nothing to do with you!

FILE. *(Right of her. Impulsively—with deep feeling)*
It's got a lot to do with me! Tell me!

(Suddenly we hear the voice of STARBUCK. *He is outdoors, approaching, singing at the top of his voice.
A quick, sharp stir in the room.)*

LIZZIE. *(Runs to kitchen. Shouting desperately)* Starbuck—go away!—run!

(His singing continues, closer.)

LIZZIE. *(Wildly as the singing continues)* Starbuck—
run!

*(*NOAH *gets down Left corner.* STARBUCK *enters through
the Right door. His pace is so rapid that he comes
full into the room, still singing.* FILE *slams the door
shut—and* STARBUCK *is confronted with* FILE'S
drawn gun.)

LIZZIE. *(To* STARBUCK*)* I told you to run!

STARBUCK. *(Center.)* What's goin' on?

FILE. *(Right.)* Sheriff! You're under arrest.
(As STARBUCK *moves.)*
Don't go for that door!

LIZZIE. If you hadn't been singing, you'd have heard
me!

STARBUCK. I never regret singin'— All right, Sheriff,
let's go!

LIZZIE. *(In an outcry)* File, wait a minute—let him
go!

FILE. What??

LIZZIE. Let him get away!!

FILE. I can't do that, Lizzie! *(Showing her "wanted" circular)* Look at this bulletin!

H.C. *(Suddenly; to Left Center.)* We don't have to look at that! We've been looking at him!

FILE. This is all I have to go by, H.C.!

JIM. *(On stairs Left.)* You've got us to go by, File! We spent the whole evenin' with this fella!

H.C. We gave him a hundred dollars—and we'll never regret a nickel of it!

JIM. He's not a criminal!

H.C. He don't belong in jail!

FILE. *(With a sense of being stampeded)* Now wait a minute!

LIZZIE. *(To FILE)* We took a chance with *him*, File! Now *you* take a chance with *us!!*

STARBUCK. *(Center.)* Give up, folks. A sheriff's a sheriff—and he can't see any further than his badge!

(FILE *flinches and* LIZZIE *hurries to him.)*

LIZZIE. *(Confronting him squarely)* Is that true, File?

FILE. You know damn well it's not true!

LIZZIE. Then let him go!

JIM. Please! Let him go!

FILE. *(Crosses Left to* NOAH. *After the smallest instant —looking at* NOAH) Haven't heard a word from you, Noah. There'd be a lot of people around here who'd think I was breakin' the law. Right?

NOAH. *(At Left end of sofa. After a struggle with himself)* Nobody I know of.

FILE. *(Around to back of sofa. Quickly to* STAR-BUCK) All right, get goin'! Get out of here!

STARBUCK. Well, I'm a son of a gun! *(He rushes to the door and stops on the threshold.)*

FILE. Hurry up before I change my mind!!

STARBUCK. *(In door. Desperately)* Lizzie—it's as lonely as dyin' out there—will you come with me?!

LIZZIE. *(Right Center. Amazed—unable to handle the sudden offer.)* Starbuck—

STARBUCK. I'm talkin' to you, Lizzie! Come on!

(She takes a step toward him—tentative, frightened. Suddenly, out of the tense stillness—FILE's voice! The words he was never able to say tear out of him in a tortured cry:)

FILE. *(To Left of table.)* Lizzie—don't go!!!

LIZZIE. *(She turns and looks at him, stunned, unable to believe it is FILE's voice.)* What—what did you say?

FILE. I said don't go!!

LIZZIE. Oh, what'll I do?!

STARBUCK. Hurry up, Lizzie—please!

LIZZIE. *(Caught between the two men, LIZZIE glances wildly around the room.)* Pop, what am I going to do?!

H.C. *(Left Center.)* Whatever you do, remember you been asked! You don't never have to go through life a woman who ain't been asked!

STARBUCK. I'm sure askin'! Lizzie, listen! You're beautiful now, but you come with me and you'll be so beautiful, you'll light up the world!

LIZZIE. *(Frightened)* No—don't say that!

STARBUCK. *(He cannot be stopped.)* You'll never be Lizzie no more—you'll be—you'll be Melisande!

LIZZIE. *(With a cry that is part lament, part relief)* Oh, Starbuck, you said the wrong thing!

FILE. Melisande? What the hell does that mean? Her name's Lizzie Curry!

STARBUCK. It's not good enough—not for her!

FILE. It's good enough for me!

STARBUCK. *(To LIZZIE.)* Come on!

LIZZIE. No—I've got to be *Lizzie!* Melisande's a name for one night—but Lizzie can do me my whole life long!

(She turns away from him. Her decision has been made. STARBUCK tries to hide the deep desperation. He tries to smile, to be the braggart again. He addresses the CURRY MEN with a bravura shout.)

STARBUCK. Well, boys! I'm sorry about the rain—but then I didn't stay my full time! So there's your hundred dollars! *(He tosses the bundle of money up in the air.)* *(JIM catches it.)*
Another day maybe—in a dry season! So long, folks! *(And he's out in a streak of dust.)*

LIZZIE. Thank you, File, thank you.

FILE. *(Studying her)* Well!—You've got your hair down!

JIM. Yep! She sure has changed!

(FILE *takes a step toward her. They look at each other closely. He smiles—the first full, radiant smile we've seen on his face. And the warmth of it shines on* LIZZIE—*and she starts to smile too— Suddenly a sound in the distance—a quick, low RUMBLE.)*

NOAH. *(Left. Hearing the sound; not watching* JIM.) Jimmy, for Pete sake, stop beatin' that drum!

JIM. I ain't beatin' no drum!

(They ALL *look at* JIM. *He is yards away from* STAR-BUCK'S *drum. Another RUMBLE is heard.)*

H.C. *(Unable to believe what he hears.)* That sounds like— *(With a shout)* It's thunder!

(A streak of LIGHTNING flashes the lights, dimming the room and electrifying it at the same time.)

JIM. Lightning!

H.C. *Light—ning!*

FILE. Look at it! It's gonna rain!

JIM. He said twenty-four hours—he said twenty-four hours!

(More LIGHTNING, more THUNDER.)

LIZZIE. *(In highest exaltation)* It's going to rain! Rain!

(Suddenly Starbuck *stands on the threshold—with a look of glory on his face.)*

Starbuck. Rain, folks—it's gonna rain! Lizzie—for the first time in my life—rain! *(Turning to* Jim*)* Gimme my hundred dollars! *(As* Jim *joyously gives him the money,* Starbuck *rushes to the door and turns to* Lizzie *only long enough to say:)* So long—beautiful! *(And he races out.)*

END OF ACT THREE

THE RAINMAKER

PROPERTY PLOT

ACT ONE

Table C.—27 x 48
5 chairs (one a low-backed captain's chair C.)
Small sofa (and hassock)
Chest seat—containing quilt and 6 napkins
Table cloth in kitchen
Clothes rack on wall above door
Cupboard
Small table L.C.
Small stand up R. with crystal set radio hooked up to
    old phonograph horn
Table service for nine (at least): silver, plates, cups,
    saucers, serving dishes, etc.
Table cloths
Bread, jam (in pint mason jar), sugar, salt, pepper,
    creamer, butter, etc.
Coffee pot
Water pitcher (porcelain or earthenware)
12 tumblers
2 frying pans (black, stamped iron skillets)
Glass water pitcher
Glass jar for silver
Ash trays
Pan of water in sink
Towels—utility and kitchen towels
Large tray for clearing dishes from table, etc.
10 (?) fried eggs—2 raw eggs off L.
Fried potatoes
Kitchen utensils—bread knife, mixing spoons, cake-
    turners, etc.

Soiled apron (high, butcher's type for H.C.)

2 pot holders, trivet

Housewife's apron for Lizzie

Curtains on windows at sink

Calendar on wall with pencil on string on rear wall Left of window

Glass bowl of fruit (grapes, special)

Steak and kidney pie in serving dish—not eaten

12 biscuits on tray or plate with napkin cover

Book (Trilby)

Magazines, newspapers (small town), and catalogs

2 bookkeeping ledgers (used), pen, ink, blotter, pencils on cupboard

Cigar box containing checkers and a checker board (old and used)

2 farm lanterns (one practical). 1 off L. and 1 hanging on nail in tack room.

2 saddles, 1 saddle bag (single) in tack room

Pieces of harness hanging on wall of tack room

Buggy seat in tack room

Nail keg in tack room

Old tin funnel—5 inch

Old commercial cardboard fan off L. (Lizzie)

Farming tools in tack room

Wagon wheel in tack room

2 upright phones, 1 on File's desk; 1 on table foot of stairs L.

Towel on nail outside window

Gifts scattered on floor L.C.—boxes and wrappings, string and tissue for a fountain pen, horsehair hat band, and tooled leather belt (with large shiny buckle)— all new

Large thermometer on porch

Door slam L.

Suitcase (Lizzie's); some of her clothes still in it after unpacking—jacket, petticoat, skirt, dressing-gown, etc. (on floor)

Newspaper, and 5 or 6 pieces of mail (circulars) off L. (H.C.)

Jack knife (H.C.)
Pipe, rubber pouch, tobacco, matches (H.C.)
Pocket watch with old leather fob for Noah (braided
    leather?)
Eyeshade for Noah (bookkeeper's or station master's
    type)
Short hickory stick (special)
Box of penny matches for H.C. (not safety)

FILE'S OFFICE

Roll-top desk with blotter, ink, pens, pencils, note-pads,
Bulletins, circulars, etc.
Swivel chair
2 stools
Leather couch
Legal notices, police bulletins with photos, etc.
Spittoon
Clock
5 or 6 large books (law, or annual county records, etc.)
Battered coffee pot
Cigar box containing needles, thread, buttons, pins,
    straight razor, tooth brush (old)
Razor strop
Shoe shine rag
Ash trays
Newspaper off R. for Sheriff
Mirror for shaving—lather—strop-razor

ACT TWO

Small black metal money box with key and practical lock
$100—8 tens, 4 fives
Extra large bass drum with several mallets
Bowl of fruit (grapes)
Some pieces (servings) of lemon cake
Rags (floor) off R. on porch for H.C. to wipe up paint
4 feed sacks in tack room back of buggy seat, filled
    with sawdust (Starbuck makes bed of these)
Pitchman's chart of zodiac (4' x 7')

Circus lantern
Towel, white wash brush and bucket of white paint off
    L. for H.C.
Note pad with writing
2 pairs of socks (File's) drying on string across his window

ACT THREE

Revolver in sideboard drawer
Package of $100 (Starbuck)
2 panatellas off L. for Jimmy
Small red hat (special) for Jimmy
Slip of paper, 2 guns, handcuffs, off L. for File and
    Sheriff
Hairpins for Lizzie's pockets
Post-card photo
Klaxon

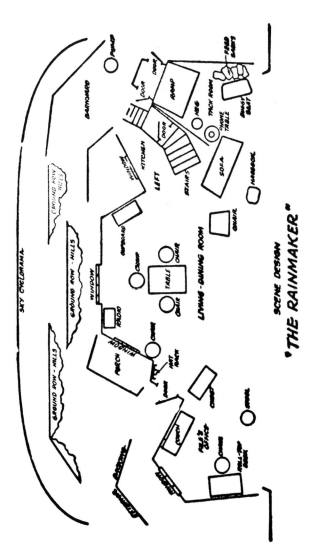

SCENE DESIGN

"THE RAINMAKER"

OTHER TITLES AVAILABLE FROM SAMUEL FRENCH

EVIL DEAD: THE MUSICAL
Book & Lyrics By George Reinblatt
Music By Frank Cipolla/Christopher Bond/Melissa Morris/
George Reinblatt

Musical Comedy / 6m, 4f / Unit set

Based on Sam Raimi's 80s cult classic films, *Evil Dead* tells the tale of 5 college kids who travel to a cabin in the woods and accidentally unleash an evil force. And although it may sound like a horror, its not! The songs are hilariously campy and the show is bursting with more farce than a Monty Python skit. *Evil Dead: The Musical* unearths the old familiar story: boy and friends take a weekend getaway at abandoned cabin, boy expects to get lucky, boy unleashes ancient evil spirit, friends turn into Candarian Demons, boy fights until dawn to survive. As musical mayhem descends upon this sleepover in the woods, "camp" takes on a whole new meaning with uproarious numbers like "All the Men in my Life Keep Getting Killed by Candarian Demons," "Look Who's Evil Now" and "Do the Necronomicon."

Outer Critics Circle nomination for
Outstanding New Off-Broadway Musical

"The next Rocky Horror Show!"
- New York Times

"A ridiculous amount of fun."
- Variety

"Wickedly campy good time."
- Associated Press